OUTLAW ON HORSEBACK

Will Ermine

CENTER POINT LARGE PRINT
THORNDIKE, MAINE

This Center Point Large Print edition
is published in the year 2016 by arrangement with
Golden West Literary Agency.

First US edition: Doubleday & Company, Inc.
First UK edition: Sampson Low

The text of this Large Print edition is unabridged.
In other aspects, this book may vary
from the original edition.

Set in 16-point Times New Roman type.

ISBN: 978-1-62899-841-2 (hardcover)
ISBN: 978-1-62899-846-7 (paperback)

Library of Congress Cataloging-in-Publication Data

Names: Ermine, Will, 1888–1979.
Title: Outlaw on horseback / Will Ermine.
Description: Center Point Large Print edition. | Thorndike, Maine :
Center Point Large Print, 2016. | ©1946
Identifiers: LCCN 2015038574 | ISBN 9781628998412
        (hardcover : alk. paper)
Subjects: LCSH: Outlaws—Fiction. | Large type books. | GSAFD:
Western stories.
Classification: LCC PS3507.R1745 O94 2016 | DDC 813/.54—dc23
LC record available at http://lccn.loc.gov/2015038574

Printed and bound in Great Britain
by TJ International Ltd, Padstow, Cornwall

MIX
Paper from
responsible sources
FSC® C013056
FSC
www.fsc.org

LIST OF CHAPTERS—

I	A Neatly Staged Bank Robbery	7
II	One Prize Quarry	23
III	An Encounter on Neutral Ground	38
IV	Outwitted	56
V	An Altered Decision	67
VI	Belle Shows Her Hand	85
VII	"Let's Ride!"	100
VIII	Holed Up	115
IX	Eight Minus Three	127
X	Feminine Trigger Finger	137
XI	A Mission of Mercy	149
XII	Death Intercedes	163
XIII	Casing the Layout	173
XIV	Squaring an Old Grudge	186
XV	Win or Lose All	202
XVI	A Fight to the Finish	213
XVII	In Lifetime Legal Custody	227

Chapter One:
A NEATLY STAGED BANK ROBBERY

DAD FINNEY, the Rock Island conductor, a slender, spindle-shanked little man, darted across the open platform between the baggage car and the smoker on the speeding train. The wind caught him and he seemed to pop into the half-filled coach. He dragged his right leg a little, and the lurching of the car accentuated the handicap he had suffered when the Doolin gang held up his train at Waukomis, two years back, and a slug from an outlaw gun had almost cost him the leg.

Dad made his way down the aisle of the swaying car and sat down with one of his passengers, his habitually harried, complaining look a little sharper than usual.

"Ed's doin' the best he can, Dick," he grumbled, "but you couldn't nurse better than thirty-five miles an hour out of that old boiler if the devil was behind you and you could feel his breath on yore heels. 'Bout eleven miles to Manatee now. We ought to roll in in twenty minutes."

"That'll be all right," was the complacent answer. "A few minutes more or less can't make any difference. The bank was robbed two hours ago. I don't expect to find the boys who pulled the job waiting around for me to get there."

The other passengers had swung around in their seats and were straining their ears to catch what was being said. They were mostly ranchers and small-town businessmen, and they knew the tall, lean-faced man, still in his early thirties, was Dick Marr, deputy United States marshal for northern Oklahoma. His quiet manner and the promise of a smile that hovered on his wide, generous mouth hardly suggested that he had already made a formidable reputation for himself as a successful man hunter. But the record said otherwise; he had taken a leading part in smashing Red Doolin's Wild Bunch and had brought the Yeager gang and other redoubtable outlaws to the end of their tether.

"I allus figgered Manatee was one town that was safe as long as Rufe Perry was patrollin' it," Dad declared weightily. "Banks have been hoisted all over this country, but even Doolin gave Manatee a wide berth. You got any idea who pulled this trick, Dick?"

The marshal shook his head.

"I could name a dozen that the job would fit."

The answer disappointed Dad; he wanted to have more to tell on his run north than just that the Manatee bank had been robbed.

"She's a rich little town," he began again, hoping to draw the marshal out. "That bank must've been crammed full of money. How much did they git away with, Dick?"

A smile played along Marr's mouth and his gray

eyes twinkled. "I'm not holding back on you, Dad. I wish there was something I could tell you. All I know is what Rufe wired me. He just said the bank had been robbed and asked me to come at once. He was lucky to catch me at Bowie. In another hour I would have been on my way south to Kingfisher and Guthrie."

The old man seemed to realize he had been told the truth and that it was idle to try to drag any further information out of the marshal. He subsided for a minute or two before he said soberly, "I hate to see you take up this trail alone. God knows where it'll take you. You've allus been lucky, but there's such a thing as a man crowdin' his luck too hard. Where's them two side kicks of yores?"

"Huck Isbell and Lafe Roberts?" Marr queried, mentioning the two field marshals with whom he had worked for three years.

"I wouldn't be meanin' no one else," Dad snapped. "Lord knows you'd never have come out of that big fight at Ingalls alive if it hadn't been for them."

Marr's smile fled, and he pulled down the corners of his mouth. "No one knows that better than I," he said simply. "I won't be surprised if I find them waiting for me in Manatee. They're either there or coming across country from Wahuska on the double-quick. I was able to get word to them in a hurry."

Dad perked up with a deduction of his own.

"Strange, all three of you bein' up in this part of the country. Sounds like you must've got wind that this was comin' off."

"No, it was something else, Dad."

The train thundered across Owl Creek, and a few minutes later the engineer was blowing for Manatee. Dad walked back to the door with the marshal.

"I wish you the best of luck, Dick. Don't have no mercy on 'em if you catch up with 'em. I didn't have any money in that bank and it wa'n't my money the Doolins took out of the express car that time at Waukomis, but I got a grudge ag'in all outlaws for what one of 'em did to me. Oklahoma ain't goin' to amount to shucks till they're all killed off!"

Marr swung down to the platform as the train rolled into Manatee. It was still just an ugly, treeless one-street town, though as Oklahoma towns went it was old, for in the not-too-long ago the old Texas Trail had uncoiled its long miles through Manatee and provided the reason for its existence. The tawny ruts, ground deep into the prairie sod, were still there, but the legions of longhorns and the brawling crews that brought them up from the Panhandle were only a memory now.

Rufe Perry, the marshal of the town, his face ruddy behind his wide white mustache, was there to meet him. They walked away hurriedly, not saying anything until they were beyond the depot.

"This job was figgered mighty neat," Rufe growled. He took the robbery as a personal affront to himself, and though the crime had been committed in the early afternoon he was still bristling with anger. "They caught me out at my farm, three miles from town. I don't go out more'n once or twice a month. Somebody tipped 'em off to it, and they waited until they had me out of the way."

"Who was it, Rufe?" Marr asked, with a marked absence of excitement.

"Britt Morgan! A hundred people saw him! He didn't light a shuck for Mexico after Doolin and Bill Dalton was killed and you fellas figgered the gang was busted up. Or if he did, he's back, and big as life! There was seven of 'em altogether. I can name 'em for you."

The marshal's mouth tightened perceptibly. "Britt, eh?" he said, and his tone gave little indication of his genuine surprise. "I figured he was too smart to come back and try to pick up where he left off. The country has changed some; he'll find that stopping trains and robbing banks is no longer a profitable business."

"Hunh! I don't know about that!" Rufe snorted. "They walked off with at least twenty thousand dollars this afternoon, and you can put two and two together and be awful certain it was Morgan

11

and his bunch who pulled that little job over on the Santa Fe two weeks ago. That night's work netted them eighty-five hundred in gold and currency. That's purty good for a beginnin'. Britt Morgan ain't no small-time outlaw; he learned his trade from a past master at the business. He's always been smart as a fox. Reckon if the truth was known he was as much the boss of the Wild Bunch as Doolin. Every lone-wolf outlaw between here and the Panhandle will come arunnin' if he just whistles!"

Marr nodded. "I never underestimated Britt. He's a leader. I don't doubt for a second that he's been able to rally a gang around him that'll be hard to curry. But they'll be stopped and come to the same bloody end as the Daltons and Doolin and all the others. Who's he got riding with him, Rufe?"

Rufe Perry pursed his lips and shook his head gravely, as a man will who is impressed by what he is about to say. "There ain't no unknowns among 'em," he said heavily. "There's Link Mulvey, Frank Cherry, Buck Younger—" He paused to flick a glance at Dick to see how he was taking it, for he had named three men against whom the law had half a hundred grudges; desperate, reckless men—Link Mulvey, one of the last of the old-time cowboy outlaws who had defied Judge "Hanging" Parker in his courtroom in Fort Smith and miraculously escaped the gallows; Frank Cherry, who had been a boy outlaw with Quantrell; Buck Younger, the wild man, who refused to sleep with a roof over his head and whose guns were literally covered with notches.

"That ought to give you an idea of it," Rufe continued. "He's got that pock-faced runt, the Tulsa Kid, with him, and Reb Santee and Arkansaw Bob."

Dick Marr's face had thinned and taken on a hard, flat look. As Rufe had said, there were no unknowns, no novices at outlawry in that gang. These men were the remnants of half a dozen gangs that he and his field marshals, and other peace officers, had broken up or scattered, welded together now in a formidable organization. In the course of the incessant warfare the law waged against those who lived outside it, it was usual when an outlaw gang began to disintegrate for the man or two who escaped death or prison to join up with some other gang or form one of their own. But for the survivors of half a dozen lawless bands to throw in together like this was something that had never happened before.

"It's a tough bunch," the marshal admitted grimly. "Not a one of them but has smelled a lot of gun smoke in his time. Maybe finding them running together this way goes to prove what I said a minute ago."

"Just how?" Rufe inquired stolidly.

"That they know as well as I do that the days of organized banditry in Oklahoma are numbered. Those old hands like Link Mulvey and Frank Cherry must realize they can't go it alone any more and beat the law for long. I can't imagine any other reason that'd make them throw in with Morgan and take orders from him. Have you seen anything of Isbell and Roberts?"

"No! I didn't know they was comin'. They ridin' in?"

"From Wahuska."

"They may be up at the bank. Been half an hour since I went down to wait for you. You want to go straight up to the bank?"

"No, we'll stop at your office. It'll save time; you know what happened, and I can get the facts from you in a few minutes."

Rufe Perry's office occupied the front of the building, originally a grocery store, that housed the town jail. The door was open; they walked in without bothering to close it behind them.

According to Rufe's story, Morgan and his men had ridden into town at ten minutes past two that afternoon and reached the corner on which the bank stood by using a side road that came in from the west. They had left their horses at the side of the building, with the Tulsa Kid gathering up the reins. The rest had walked to the corner. Buck Younger and Arkansaw Bob had stopped there. Morgan and the others had hurried into the bank,

14

with Reb Santee taking up his position at the door.

"Was there any shooting up to that point?" the marshal inquired.

"No, not a gun popped. The town was taken by surprise. You know how that goes. Everybody knew it was a raid; the first thing they did was to get off the street. I'd always figgered that if anything like this happened, the best way to break it up was from the roof of the hotel, across the street from the bank. I'd often talked it over with Cleve Brown, my constable. He rounded up a couple men and they started for the hotel by way of the back alley. It must have taken them some time to get on the hotel roof. Morgan and his men were inside the bank fully ten minutes, accordin' to all accounts. When they walked in, they found four customers standing at the counter. Link Mulvey lined them up. Britt stuck up the cashier and Streeter. Frank Cherry leaped over the counter and got busy at the open safe. They had it planned like clockwork. Nick Rowan's pointer dog wandered in. Reckon things was so quiet it scared him. He stood in the door, barkin' his fool head off."

Marr was familiar with the pattern of such moments. "Guns usually begin cracking about that time," he observed casually.

"They did—all along the street! But you know what kind of shootin' that was, Dick. Nobody was exposing himself; just makin' a lot of noise.

Cherry had scooped up everythin' in sight. He started for the door and Mulvey and Morgan started backin' out. They had just reached Santee when a burst of shots came from the hotel roof. It was Cleve. He claims he dropped Buck Younger with his first shot. He saw the old blackleg floppin' around on the sidewalk till he rolled in back of the water trough on the corner. Arkansaw Bob stood there with the slugs whinin' around him and shot Cleve's rifle out of his hands. There was a clerk from the hardware store—Homer Bruce, if you know him—up there with Cleve. Big Arkansaw winged him too. That ended the shootin' from the roof. They tell me Britt and the rest of 'em just stood there in front of the bank then, spatterin' shots right and left. Nobody was gittin' hurt, but it was a convincin' argument."

"It usually is," said Dick. "Have you got Younger?"

"Hell no! Morgan picked him up and set him on his horse. They was poundin' out of town a minute later, headin' west. Streeter ran out into the street, wavin' a sawed-off shotgun and yellin' for a posse and offerin' a reward. Some men got organized. They didn't go far. Morgan's crowd had hauled up in those willow brakes along Owl Crick. They expected to be pursued, and it didn't seem to worry 'em. When the posse ran into gunfire, somebody remembered that it wasn't their bank that had been robbed, and they came back to town.

16

Cleve had sent for me. When I got here everythin' was quiet, 'cept for Sam Streeter. He's still howlin'."

Marr nodded understandingly and said, "Don't let it bother you, Rufe. Thanks to you, this is the first time Streeter's bank has been touched up. I'll remind him of it if he starts throwing the gravel into me. Let's go up there."

As they neared the bank they saw two jaded horses standing at the hitchrack. Rufe ran his eyes over them.

"Looks like Isbell and Roberts have got here," he remarked. "Those broncs have come a long ways, and fast."

"Yeh," Dick murmured in his tight-lipped way.

The two field marshals had arrived, and when they saw Marr coming they stepped out of the bank; Huck Isbell, tall and angular, with a plain, unsmiling face, and Lafe Roberts, a pint-size little man, wiry and tremendously alert, and possessing a catlike gracefulness and ease of movement. Both men were well along toward 50, but Lafe's red thatch still flamed as brilliantly as ever. He was often twitted about it, some of his cronies claiming he dyed his hair, which he denied violently. They were old hands at this business, and a quiet efficiency rested on them that could not be mistaken.

"You got here, I see," said Dick. "Looks like you rode those broncs into the ground."

Lafe grinned. "We shore crowded 'em a little." He sobered quickly. "Seems we got the Doolin job to do all over ag'in, Dick."

"It does," was the terse admission. "Did you see or hear anything on the way over?"

"Not a thing," Huck answered. "They must have passed us a few miles to the south. Reckon that was jest as well," he added dryly. "If what we been hearin' here is correct, it wouldn't be healthy to run into that bunch by mistake."

They were well acquainted with Rufe Perry. After exchanging a few words with him, all four walked into the bank together. They found Sam Streeter, the banker, behind the counter, talking to a group of Manatee merchants. Streeter waved them aside on catching sight of the marshal, and though his apoplectic wrath and excitement had all but exhausted him, his eyes blazed now as he whipped himself into a trembling rage that drove the blood away from his damp face.

He was a flabby, obese man, and his tirade was punctuated with a scratchy gasping for breath. It would not have surprised Marr to see him clutch his heart and slide to the floor.

"That's about enough of that, Streeter," Dick declared bluntly. "You can't complain about the protection you've had through the years. I don't believe you'll be able to work up much sympathy for yourself by trying to hold Rufe or me responsible for this robbery."

18

"But you must have known there was something in the wind!" Streeter burst out afresh. "You marshals have got ways of hearing things; a gang like that don't get organized overnight! I don't see why you couldn't have tipped me off!"

"That train robbery at Marland a couple weeks ago was tip-off enough for most people." Marr seldom lost his temper, and he was in no danger of doing so now.

"The train crew reported only two masked men did that job. You gave that out yourself. There wasn't no talk about a big gang of cutthroats like this being on the loose! If you had reason to think there was, it was up to you to pass the information along! Maybe Perry would have been on the job this afternoon." Streeter glared at Rufe. "It might have made some difference. But Lord knows time enough has been wasted without standing here wrangling now! The thing to do is to go after those men! Ride them down and make some effort to recover my money!"

"That's nonsense, Mr. Streeter," Huck Isbell spoke up. "Yore money's gone and you got to git used to the idea. I been huntin' outlaws for years. You can kill 'em or send 'em off to the pen, but you don't git nuthin' back, no matter how much they got away with in their time. Doolin had only eighteen dollars on him when he was killed, and if he didn't git away with a hundred thousand, I'm crazy. What did Bill Dalton have left? Nuthin'!

I can name you a hundred—Belle Starr, Frank Starr, the Sontags. It's always the same; when the law catches up with 'em they're broke."

He was saying only what every man in the room knew to be a fact, Sam Streeter included. A million dollars, more or less, had been looted from Oklahoma banks, railway trains, and express offices. Little or none of it had ever been recovered. Aside from Belle Starr, the woman bandit, who, when she wasn't dodging the law, squandered a fortune on her race horses, there was no record of lavish spending by any known outlaw. What they did with the money they stole remained a mystery. It was often said that they buried it and were never able to get back to it, but though any number of industrious citizens had been digging in likely places for years, no one had ever turned up anything. It was Marr's opinion that the "tick" birds, the so-called "friends" who protected outlaws, passed information on to them, and supplied them with food and whatever else they needed, got away with most of it.

The marshal turned to Rufe. "We're going to need some horses. Can you fix us up?"

"Sure!" Rufe answered, his suddenly narrowing eyes sharp with a question beneath their hooded brows. "I hope this doesn't mean you're goin' to try to ride that bunch down."

Marr smiled thinly. "No, I don't hunt outlaws that way, Rufe, and Streeter understands it. Britt knows he and his gang will be safe enough for the present if he leads them back across the Cimarron. I just want to make sure that that's what he's doing."

"That's a fine way to handle things!" Streeter howled. "They've got a railroad to cross before they reach the river. You could make some effort to cut them off!"

"Not with the start they've got—if it's their intention to put the Cimarron behind them. You had a good look at Morgan. Was he clean-shaven?"

The banker threw up his hands in disgust, and his flabby face turned purple.

"He walks out of here with twenty-one thousand dollars, maybe a little more, and you ask me if he had whiskers on his chin! Of course he didn't! He's always been a Handsome Dan! What the hell difference can it make whether he'd run a razor over his face or not?"

"Considerable," Dick said in his quiet, tight-lipped way. "If he had led his men across the river last night and hid out somewhere west of Manatee all morning, he wouldn't have had a chance to shave. It means they moved up to the Cimarron during the night and didn't break across till after dawn."

Huck and Lafe nodded their agreement with this. They had become accustomed to having Marr pick up some trifling fact and draw startling deductions from it.

"That sounds like gospel to me," Huck remarked. "Them broncs at the rail belong to Ed West. Can you git 'em back to him, Rufe?"

Perry jerked an affirmative nod.

"I'll find some way of gittin' them over to Wahuska in the next day or two. You boys ain't got more'n three hours of daylight left. If you're goin' to make tracks, you want to git movin'. Huck, you and Lafe git them hosses down to my barn; Dick and I'll be right behind you."

They left the bank with Streeter still railing over the loss of his money and reached Rufe's barn in four or five minutes. He had half a dozen good animals in his string.

"I'll ride out as far as the crick with you and show you where they turned the posse back," he volunteered as he helped them saddle up. "Reckon you noticed that no one in the bank had a word of sympathy for Streeter. Purty hard to shed a tear for a gent that's been loanin' money at ten and twelve per cent and always ready to pull your eyeteeth if you're a day late with your interest." He slipped a rifle into his saddle boot. "Wal, if you're ready, let's go!"

"Right!" Marr answered.

They swung up easily and jogged into the yard. With Rufe leading the way, they crossed the red ribbon of dust that was the road and struck west across the open prairie.

Chapter Two:
ONE PRIZE QUARRY

IT WAS LESS than three miles to the spot on Owl Creek where Morgan and his men had convinced the hastily organized posse that further pursuit would be costly.

"Britt must have located this spot on his way in," Huck declared. "You'd hunt a long ways to find a better place to make a stand."

"They could have really forted up here if they'd had to," Rufe acknowledged. "But a posse that meant business could have come up from the rear and made things interestin', I reckon." He glanced at Marr. The latter had moved into the trees along the creek bottom and was studying the ground at his feet with obvious concern.

"What have you found, Dick?" Rufe called.

"There's blood on the ground. Looks like they performed a little buckshot surgery on Younger. They ripped up a shirt or two. Pieces lying around. They've evidently decided that Buck isn't so bad off that they can't carry him along with them."

"He's tougher than bullhide, Dick," Rufe growled. "You can't figger on him slowin' 'em up much. They'll tie him to his saddle if they have to."

Marr came back to his horse and got up. In a few

23

minutes Lafe Roberts could be heard returning from the far side of the bottoms.

"They went straight across," the little man announced. "I saw where they put their broncs up the bank. If they hold to the course they was takin', they'll cross the main line of the Rock Island somewheres between Wahuska and Woodhall. That'll put 'em in a couple miles' ridin' of the river."

"They'll make better time than that," Rufe declared, as Lafe climbed into his saddle. "They'll keep on movin' till they're 'way out in the Strip. They can hole up 'most anywheres out in that wild country and thumb their noses at you. Every squatter and hillbilly will be on their side, same as they was on Red Doolin's side."

"Sure," Marr agreed. "But there are no banks out there for them to rob, Rufe; they'll be heading back this way, sooner or later. We'll try to be ready for them. In the meantime, maybe we can stir them up a little." He raised his hand and said, "So long!"

Rufe nodded and watched them disappear in the trees before he turned back. Behind him he could hear the snapping of dry brush as the three men crossed the bottoms. Suddenly it was quiet again along the creek, and he knew they had reached the prairie.

To the north of Owl Creek there were low hills. Marr and his two deputies turned away from them and rode toward the westering sun. Though it was only mid-April, the bluejoint grass was already high enough to spread an undulating carpet before them that rose and fell to the stirring of the wind. The redbud was in bloom. Wherever the eye turned there were bright scarlet patches of it, so red that, at a distance, against the blue of the sky, it seemed as though the prairie were aflame.

Huck and Lafe rode along with eyes that saw nothing of the beauty of the spring afternoon. The reverse was true with Dick Marr. Though he was Kentucky-born, this was his country and he loved its various moods, its wide horizons and the wild tang of its prairies, even its loneliness. He knew the day must come when this land would be fenced off, the grass plowed under, and the business of living made as orderly as it was in the states back across the Mississippi. He was even devoting himself to bringing that day nearer. It was a wholly desirable prospect. And yet, with the wind laying its cool kiss against his face and the unbroken miles of grass stretching out ahead of him, he was filled with a vague regret for the changes that must come.

Rufe's horses were hard, and they moved along without raising a sweat. Lafe Roberts held the lead and set the pace. He pulled up sharply when he reached a low rise. He pointed off to the right. A column of smoke was curling up from the chimney of a dugout.

"Family of nesters in there, Dick," he said. "You want to stop?"

"We better, Lafe. There's no reason to think we'll have trouble there, but we'll look the place over carefully before we ride in."

They pulled up when they were several hundred yards from the dugout.

"Don't see any hosses," Huck observed. "Flock of kids playin' in the yard. These people have kids when they don't have nuthin' else."

"Let's go up to the door," said Dick.

A thin, tired-looking woman stepped out to meet them. She twisted her scraggly hair into a knot on top of her head.

"Where's your man?" Marr asked.

"Paw's up the draw lookin' fer our caow," she replied, her eyes suspicious. "Yo're the law, I reckon," she added on catching sight of the shield Huck wore.

"That's right," Isbell told her. "We ain't aimin' to make you no trouble if you'll give us a straight answer to a couple questions. A bunch of men passed here this afternoon. What did they have to say?"

"Say?" the woman demanded indignantly. "Reckon yo're mistaken, mister! They didn't turn in yere. They was half a mile out on the prairie. The childurn saw 'em or we'd never noticed 'em at all."

"Which way was they movin'?" Lafe inquired.

"Ridin' west. What was they, outlaws?"

"Wal, they wasn't a bunch of Baptist preachers goin' to a convention," Lafe said dryly. He glanced at Marr, and the marshal took over.

"Where do you keep your horses?" he asked.

"We only got the one. Paw's ridin' him. He allus does when the caow strays and he has to go lookin' fer her. Cynthy, you stop pullin' my apron!" The children, one of them barely old enough to toddle, were crowding around her nervously. They were a ragged brood, with the half-starved look of youngsters who seldom see anything more nourishing than hominy grits and a little sorghum. "The flock of you go play and let me talk to these men!"

There was a patch of plowed ground below the dugout. A plow stood in an unfinished furrow. A work harness had been carelessly dropped over the handles. The upturned soil in the furrow was still moist. It convinced Marr that the woman's story about her husband having taken the horse and gone off to look for the cow was the truth.

"How long have you been living here?" he questioned.

"Better'n three years."

"And the name?"

"Slemp—Jotham Slemp. We're poor, but we're honest folks, if I do say it."

"I'm sorry we had to bother you," said Dick. "We'll get along." He touched the brim of his

Stetson and rode out of the yard, with Huck and Lafe falling in behind him.

They were a quarter of a mile from the dugout before they came abreast.

"I don't know whether that old gal was lyin' to us or not," Lafe grumbled skeptically. "I couldn't find no fresh hoss tracks in the yard; but that don't prove nothin'—not with a cute customer like Morgan. He could have turned up the draw with Slemp's help. Trapper's Crick heads somewheres north of here. They could follow it all the way to the river."

"I thought she told us a straight story," said Marr.

He explained his reasons for thinking so.

"Britt's carrying a badly wounded man with him," he continued. "Trapper's Creek would put him across the Cimarron north of Wahuska and add a dozen miles to the riding he's got to do. He's not apt to make any mistakes like that. Not any doubt left in my mind that he's making for the river. He's got the railroad in his way. He can't do otherwise than figure if we're going to make him any trouble it will be there, and that the sooner he reaches the tracks, the better his chances will be."

"Yeh," Huck Isbell muttered. "That sounds like sense to me. Suppose we stir these broncs up a little. They can take it."

They quickened their pace and had little to say as they put the miles behind them. The prairie lost its flatness and began to spread out before them in low, rolling swells. They would top a rise and disappear into the dip beyond it for minutes before they reappeared on the succeeding ridge. There was nothing in the wide, shallow draws to slow them up appreciably, but their view was cut off, and from one rise to the next they had no way of knowing what they were riding into. It was dangerous and they realized it.

The sun was getting low when Marr motioned for Huck and Lafe to pull up. For some minutes they had been trying to skirt a long ravine. Ahead of them the floor of the prairie was cut up with deep gullies and crumbling cut-banks. Rain that fell here found its way to the Cimarron, and unchecked erosion had ravished the land.

"It looks worse than when I saw it last," said Marr.

Huck and Lafe nodded; they were as familiar with this section of Oklahoma as he.

"The runoff tore things up for fair," Huck declared. "We won't help ourselves none if we git tangled up in that mess. We can swing off to the south and git around it. Reckon that's what Morgan did."

"Most likely," Dick agreed. "There's a ranch or two in that direction where they could get a fresh horse if they needed one. They may be able to tell us something at the Turkey Track or Circle V."

Lafe Roberts shook his head dubiously. "If we

swing off that far, we'll find ourselves astraddle the old Bowie-Wahuska road. We don't have to do that to git around these badlands. I don't believe Morgan did."

"You'll find him doing the unexpected whenever he can," said Marr. "I'm sure he wouldn't follow the road; but he could cut it and reach the Rock Island main line about four to five miles north of Woodhall. He'd be nearer to the river there than anywhere else. We could take a chance on it."

"It's a long gamble," Huck muttered, his homely face screwed up into a thoughtful squint. "We've got only one guess comin' to us. If we're wrong, we'll be stuck with it."

"I know it," Marr acknowledged. It called for a decision, and he didn't hesitate. "We'll take a chance and play it that way. If it turns out that it was a mistake, it won't be the first one I've made."

At the Turkey Track ranch, no one had seen anything of Morgan and his men. They had better luck at Chris Hatton's Circle V.

"I wouldn't say it was Morgan, or how many there was in the bunch—I was too far away for that—but I sure saw some riders movin' across my west range this afternoon," he told them.

"How long ago was that, Chris?" Marr asked.

"Oh—two hours ago, I'd say. I didn't think too much about it; I figured it was just a bunch of cowboys goin' into Bowie. They certainly was makin' for the Bowie road. I don't mind tellin' you I'm glad I didn't let my curiosity get the better of me," he finished with a chuckle.

"You didn't see them turn into the road?"

"No, I lost sight of them long before that. There's three or four families of Arkansaw razorbacks dug in between me and the river. If you're ridin' that way you might learn somethin' from them. Then again, you might not; bein' ignorant and worthless, they wouldn't do the law a favor if they could. I've threatened to shoot the next one of 'em I catch trespassin' on my range. I know they've been gettin' away with some of my beef."

"Trash of that kind will sell a man out for a two-bit piece!" Huck growled. "Be a waste of breath to try to git anythin' out of 'em. I never knew one to have gumption enough to make an honest livin'. They'd rather peddle a little homemade corn likker and take it easy the rest of the time. The sun's down, Dick. If we're goin' to have a look at the road, we better be movin'!"

Marr nodded, and they pulled away. Twenty-five minutes later they stood on the Bowie road. Little Lafe was the first to locate the spot where Morgan and his gang had turned in and ridden west.

"They was movin' right along," he said, after studying the tracks for several minutes. "Yore hunch stood up, Dick, but I don't know what

31

good it's goin' to do us; they've got clear sailin'.."

A faint, amused smile ran along Marr's mouth.

"I wasn't hoping to overhaul them," he said. "For the present, I'll be satisfied to know we've chased them across the river. The trick is going to be to keep them there till we can figure out some way to trip them. We'll just jog along now; it shouldn't be difficult to find where they left the road."

They padded on in the dust for half a mile or less, when Lafe flung up a hand again and they reined in.

"There their tracks go!" the little man growled, pointing off across the prairie. "Looks like they was figgerin' to slip through above Woodhall, shore enough! Their hosses have knocked down the grass some; we can follow their trail easy enough as long as the light lasts."

"There's daylight enough left to git us to the railroad," Huck asserted. "It can't be more'n two miles to the ranch road that winds up from Woodhall to Wahuska. Another mile and a half and we'll hit the Rock Island."

"Maybe we won't have to go quite that far," said Marr. "If we find they're movin' west after they cross the Woodhall road, we can be sure they're heading out into the Strip. Let's go!"

As Lafe said, the trail was easily followed. When they came through some low hills, they had the little-used Woodhall road in front of them. A springless farm wagon, moving in the direction of Woodhall, had just passed. The box of the wagon was filled with loose hay. The team was moving at a walk. The driver, a thin, stringy-looking man, clad in butternut jeans and a linsey shirt, sat hunched over on the seat and gave no indication that he had seen the three horsemen who had emerged from the hills.

"One of those razorbacks Chris Hatton was tellin' us about, I reckon," Huck drawled contemptuously. "Shall we hail him, Dick?"

"No, let him go. He's pretending awfully hard that he hasn't seen us. We'll cross the road without giving him any reason to think we're interested and keep right on to the west until we've topped that rise over there. We'll turn back then and watch him for a minute or two."

They filed over the height of land below the road, only a matter of several hundred yards, and disappeared from view. Without dismounting, they swung their horses and peered cautiously over the crest. The driver of the wagon was lashing his mules into a gallop.

"I thought that would fetch him!" Marr jerked out. "It's suspicious enough to interest me. Look out for him. When he sees us closing in, he may draw a gun."

They overtook the wagon and called on the driver to pull up. The man sucked on his ragged mustache and eyed them with an uneasy hostility.

"What you runnin' yore team that-a-way for?" Huck demanded accusingly.

"I didn't like the looks of you fellas," the man returned. "I didn't see you wuz marshals. Bein' as how it's unusual to run into anyone along here, I allowed I better use the whip."

Marr questioned him and learned that his name was Lem Shoup; that he lived on Caddo Creek and was on his way into Woodhall for supplies.

"You ole buzzard, yo're lyin' from here to Sunday!" little Lafe ripped out angrily. "Nobody livin' on Caddo Crick is settin' out for town when they know the store will be closed before they git there! Yore story about bein' scared of us stickin' you up don't hold water neither, 'less you've got somethin' in this wagon you don't want us to see!"

"I wa'n't scairt," Shoup protested. "But I'm a man what minds his own business; I don't aim to see nuthin' that don't consarn me."

"Get down," Dick told him. "Keep an eye on him, Lafe; Huck and I'll have a look in the wagon."

He walked around to the endgate and started to open it. As he did, the loose hay moved violently and the haggard face and shoulders of a man appeared. His hand whipped up and he leveled a gun at Marr.

Isbell, climbing over a rear wheel, reached out and knocked the man's arm down. He tried to bring it up again, but he was so weak that he fell back helplessly. Huck yanked the gun out of his fingers.

"By cripes, it's Buck Younger!"

"Yeh," Marr monotoned. He had recognized the old outlaw instantly.

Lafe turned his wrath loose on the unhappy Lem Shoup.

"What you got to say about this, you weasel-eyed scarecrow?" he rapped violently.

"They stopped to my place and offered me fifty dollars to git this fella to a doctor. I allowed as how I could use the money. I didn't ask no questions—"

"Don't bother with him, Lafe," Dick called. "Just hang on to the mules."

Huck and he had climbed into the wagon and were tossing out the hay that covered the outlaw. The former found a rifle on the floor boards.

"He shore was all set to give us an argument," he muttered. Younger watched them, unmoved, though he was in great pain.

"You're in tough shape, Buck," the marshal said.

"Yuh couldn't have snagged me, otherwise. I got a slug layin' up ag'in my spine that's drivin' me crazy. Don't stand here runnin' at the jaw; yuh git me in to a doctor, Dick."

Marr nodded; there was no personal quarrel between him and the men he hunted.

"We'll take you in to Doc Wasson, in Woodhall.

I've got a flask of rye whisky in my saddlebag. You better have a shot; you look as though you could use it."

He got the flask and held it to Buck's lips. Gratitude flowed into the latter's hard-bitten eyes briefly.

"I've stopped a lot of lead in my day, but this is the first time I ever felt it," he said, his tone grimly bantering. "Lord knows you boys literally shot the clothes off me, over there at Ingalls. Pierce City wasn't any picnic either. I was shakin' slugs out of my hide fer a couple days after that ruckus."

"Well, this will put you on the shelf for a long time," Dick told him. "There's a flock of indictments against you. Oklahoma will be a different place when you come out."

Younger laughed scornfully. "I expected better sense from you. You know there's no jail goin' to hold me."

"The Guthrie jail will hold you if I have to put a trace chain on you."

"And there won't be no foolin' about that, Buck," Isbell interjected weightily. "Yo're the man Morgan could least afford to lose. That gang don't look half so tough to me with you out of circulation."

"Aw shucks!" the old outlaw grunted disgustedly. "Yo're talkin' through yore hat, Huck! That's the best bunch of boys was ever put together. You'll raise blisters on yore hinder, chasin' 'em!" He glanced at the marshal. "Git this wagon movin', Dick! I'm sufferin'!"

Marr told Lafe to do the driving. The little man and Lem Shoup climbed up on the seat. Huck tied Lafe's horse to the endgate. When the wagon drew away, he and Dick fell in behind.

With twilight coming on, they moved toward Woodhall, long just a shipping point for Colonel Zach Woodhall's Flying W ranch and even now hardly more than a wide place in the road with its cluster of buildings.

"We got a break—a real one, Huck," Dick said thoughtfully. "I don't believe there's a square yard of the Strip or No Man's Land with which Buck Younger isn't familiar. With his help, Britt would have been able to play hide-and-seek with us for months to come."

"There's somethin' to that," Huck agreed. "Reckon Morgan wouldn't have taken a chance on sendin' him into Woodhall if there'd been any other way of gettin' him to a doctor. What are we goin' to do with Younger?"

"If Doc Wasson says it's safe to move him, we're taking him to Guthrie tonight." Marr answered without a second's hesitation. "The Rock Island has a train south about nine o'clock. I want to be sure we've got him locked up."

Chapter Three:
AN ENCOUNTER ON NEUTRAL GROUND

TO HAVE BROUGHT an outlaw of Buck Younger's prominence into any Oklahoma town would have produced an immediate excitement. Coming hard on the heels of the robbery at Manatee, news of which had long since reached Woodhall by telegraph, lifted it to thrilling drama. Doc Wasson had his office in his home. Five minutes after Isbell and Lafe carried Younger inside, the news had run all over the little town and men began to gather on the sidewalk outside.

Having been a frontier doctor for 40 years, outlaws and gunshot wounds were nothing out of the ordinary to Ab Wasson. He stepped into his waiting-room after examining Younger.

"He's in a lot of pain, and he's bled freely, but he ain't hurt much," he told Marr. "He'll feel a lot easier as soon as I remove that chunk of lead. No reason why you shouldn't take him down to Guthrie tonight if you want to. I'll have him ready for you in thirty, forty minutes."

"Good enough," said Dick. "Can your house-keeper fix the boys up with supper while they're waiting? I thought I'd ride over to the ranch; it's only a step. I don't like to be this near without dropping in for a minute."

"Go ahead," Wasson urged. "Huck and Lafe can eat supper with me when I get through. I promise you Younger won't get up and walk out."

"Maybe not," said Dick, "but I don't want him left alone for a second."

"We'll see to that," Lafe assured him. "Will you come back here, or shall we cart Buck over to the depot and look for you there?"

"Load him into Shoup's wagon and take him to the depot. You better put him in the baggage room. I'll show up in plenty time for the train. The colonel will see to it that Rufe's horses get back to Manatee."

"What about Shoup?" Huck inquired. "We holdin' him?"

"No, we might as well let him go. I'll have a little talk with him when I step out. The colonel may have some news for me; some of his crew must have been up along the river this afternoon."

Huck and Lafe nodded, and they exchanged an understanding glance as he walked out to his horse. His interest in Belle Woodhall, old Zach's daughter, was an open secret, and they knew it was to see her, rather than the hope of hearing something about the Morgan gang, that was taking him to the ranch.

The little group waiting on the sidewalk closed around Marr before he reached the wagon. He answered their questions briefly and asked them to disperse.

"We'll give you a hand if there's anythin' we can do," one offered.

Dick thanked him and said no. As they moved away, he turned to Shoup. "I want you to wait here till they bring Younger out. They'll tell you what to do. You can head for home then. But I'm putting you down in my black book, Shoup. The next time I catch you mixing up in anything like this, you're going to the jug."

The nester jerked his eyes away furtively and had nothing to say.

"Did you hear me?" Marr barked threateningly.

"Yep, I heerd yuh," Shoup whined. With a blank look on his lined face, he sat there without moving until he saw the marshal climb into his saddle and jog off.

Its brand name of Flying W was seldom used in speaking of Colonel Zach Woodhall's immense ranch, 110,000 acres of rich prairie land, and not a yard of it under fence. To Oklahomans it was just Woodhall Ranch, famous for its hospitality and good living. With its fine house, its mansard roof, surmounted by an iron railing, its stable of race horses, immense barns and other outbuildings, it bore little resemblance to the usual cow ranch. The difference only began there, for Woodhall Ranch was an institution in itself. Whoever rode into the yard, friend or stranger, inside the law or out, and whatever his business, was welcome there. It was the colonel's proud boast that no man had ever failed to find food and a bed at Woodhall. There were legendary tales of nights that he had sat down to supper with as many as 30 men at his table. But the ranch was neutral ground. When you rode in, you took off your guns. Marr had often heard the story of how Uncle Ben Small, the famous U. S. marshal, had found himself seated across the supper table from the man he had been hunting for days.

Colonel Woodhall had worn the Confederate gray. Like so many other followers of the lost cause, left penniless by the war, he had come out to what was now Oklahoma soon after the surrender at Appomattox. If he had prospered in those turbulent years it was largely because men found something in his eyes that commanded respect and obedience. He possessed a giant frame, standing six feet two in his bare feet, and though he was now in his sixties and growing portly, his hair and flowing mustache snow-white, he was still a striking figure on horseback. Oklahoma City and Guthrie counted a parade of no consequence unless Colonel Zach, seated on his white horse, was there to lead it.

Considering the hour, Dick was rather surprised to find him seated alone on the gallery, a julep glass in his hand, when he got down at the hitchrack.

"Well, it's you, Dick!" was the old man's friendly greeting. "I don't suppose I should be surprised to see you, considering the news we got this afternoon. Come up and sit down a minute and have a drink with me!"

The marshal unbuckled his gun belt as he mounted the steps to the gallery and deposited it on the bench inside the door that was provided for that purpose. He found other guns there, proof that he wasn't the colonel's only guest this evening.

"I see you've got company," he said, as he sat down. Zach nodded.

"Just a couple boys for supper. Skidmore is up from Oklahoma City. They're arranging for the Memorial Day parade already. The committee wants me to come down. I suppose I'll have to say yes."

Though his tone suggested that an obligation was being put on him, Dick surmised that the honor of being grand marshal really meant more to Zach than the price of beef.

"I don't see anyone around," Dick remarked, as the colonel filled his glass from a frosted pitcher. "Where is everybody?"

"Belle, you mean?" Zach inquired, with a chuckle.

Marr laughed and said, "I guess that's about the size of it."

"She's down at the barn, Dick. She's got them all down there with her. That fine little mare I

42

brought up from Texas for her has just foaled. Belle chased me out of the stall and won't let anyone put a hand on the little fellow. Insists on doing everything herself. There's nothing to do but hold supper until she's finished. What about that business at Manatee?"

"We picked up Buck Younger. We brought him into Woodhall just a few minutes ago. Wasson is patching him up."

They talked about the robbery and Morgan for some minutes. The colonel began to bristle.

"I can't stop them from crossing my range," he declared hotly. "But it's stepping on my toes, and I don't like it! I've never had any trouble with outlaws because I've never taken sides. I knew that was the only way I could exist here."

"That'll be good enough for Morgan," Marr said confidently. "I believe he'll be careful not to bother you."

He felt he had his answer as to whether some of Zach's crew had been up the river and caught sight of the gang.

"Did you see anything of Bill in Guthrie?" Colonel Woodhall asked. He was speaking of his son. "He's been down there for a week, throwing money away on some woman, like as not, and making a fool of himself."

"I ran into Bill the other day," Marr answered.

"Was he drunk?" Zach snapped.

"Well, he was feeling a little high. But you know

how that is, Colonel," Dick added with an indulgent smile. "A man goes to Guthrie for a big time—"

"I don't mind a young man having a big time, but it can't be all big times!" was the gruff response. Old Zach set his glass down on the table at his elbow with an angry bang. "There's such a thing as knowing when to buckle down and put your shoulder to the wheel."

"I wouldn't worry too much about it," Dick said reassuringly. "Bill's still young—"

"He's almost as old as you are!" The colonel shook his head bitterly. "I don't know. I try to find in him some of the things I see in you, Dick; they're not there. I can't open up to everybody and say what's on my mind, but I've never held anything back from you. I don't like to admit it, but Bill's a disappointment to me. Belle should have been the man in my family. I used to tell her mother that when Belle and Bill were just children." He looked away, musing to himself for a moment. "It was the only thing their mother and I ever differed about. If Belle is wilder than a hawk, it's my fault; I didn't know how to raise a girl, but I thought I knew how to bring up a boy."

Behind them an aged Negro moved through the dining-room, lighting the lamps. When he was finished, he carried his taper into the living-room and performed a similar service. The colonel called him out on the gallery.

"Is there any sign of them coming up from the barn, Ned?"

"Yas, suh, dere's signs, Colonel. Dey's got as far as de barn doh'. After a little more talkin', Ah spects dey'll be comin'." The old darky wagged his bald head. "Miss Belle sho' handle dat foal lak' no man on dis ranch could do." He bowed to Marr. "Evenin' to yuh, Mist' Dick! If yuh're stayin' de night wid us, Ah'll have yo' hoss put up."

"The marshal's taking the train south," Zach told him. "You can have the horse put up; he's leaving it here."

With an emphatic "Yas, suh!" the old Negro hurried into the house. The colonel sat there with his chin on his chest for a moment, lost in thought.

"Women are full of contradictions, Dick," he declared weightily. "Take Belle—she won't wear overalls, says it's not ladylike. Yet she'll go down to the barn and help a mare to foal and think nothing of it. It points up what I was telling you a few minutes ago; she can ride and rope with the best man on the place. She's a dead shot with a rifle or a short gun. The other day she killed a wolf with a stirrup iron. She's got so much spunk and backbone it scares me sometimes. On the other hand, you see her down in Oklahoma City and she's the prettiest, daintiest thing you ever laid eyes on."

Marr leaned back and regarded him with a

broad smile. He knew how proud Zach Woodhall was of his daughter.

"You're trying to find the answer to a riddle that's as old as the world, Colonel. It's a woman's inconsistencies that make her charming and exciting. When she's mad, Belle can use some words you won't find in the Bible, but I've never found anything in her that I'd want any different. As for you, you wouldn't change her if you could."

"No, but she's willful; she needs taming, Dick. She'd take it from you. Why don't you marry her?"

Marr's laughter was free of embarrassment.

"It's not because I haven't asked her," he said.

"Well, keep on asking her!" old Zach ordered, his voice gruff and rumbling. "If you want to clean up a bit before we go to the table, use my room; you know your way around the house. Lord knows I'm going to need someone here like you in the days to come!"

The murmur of voices crossing the rear yard reached them. Man got to his feet.

"I hear them coming now," he said, starting for the door. "I won't be more than a minute or two."

He crossed the living-room. Belle's rosewood piano stood in its accustomed place. He put out his hand and touched it affectionately, thinking of the many times he had seen her seated at the keyboard, first as a girl in her early teens, just home from her first term at Miss Milliken's Female Seminary in St. Louis, and insisting that she was never going back.

A pair of worn silver spurs, so small that they obviously were hers, had been left hanging on the sliding music rack. Marr did not find it an incongruous touch; the piano was Belle, as nothing else in the house could hope to be.

The colonel's blunt question was still ringing in his ears. A stab of hopelessness tightened his mouth and put sober lines in his face as he stood alone at the piano for a moment. Belle Woodhall held for him all that he ever hoped to find in a woman, a rich treasure beyond any man's dreaming. Because he knew it was either Belle or no one for him, he had closed his mind against any recognition of defeat. And yet the truth rested heavily on him tonight and he could not throw it off. He knew Belle was fond of him. But that wasn't enough; and it never would be.

In Zach's bedroom he scowled at his reflection in the mirror as he refreshed himself. I'm afraid I haven't dash enough for Belle, was his bitter thought. To claim her, I'd have to sweep her off her feet. If I tried anything like that I'd only make myself ridiculous. I hope I'll always have sense enough to realize it.

Someone passed the door, and he recognized Belle's quick step as she hurried down the hall. Voices in the living-room reached him. He was acquainted with every one in the little group gathered around the colonel—Gil Skidmore, the lawyer from Oklahoma City; a cattle buyer from Guthrie; Thad Taylor and Henry Goss, both well-known cowmen; and Chauncey Dibbs, the Rock Island's general freight agent. They were discussing the Manatee raid, and when Marr joined them they demanded a detailed account from him.

"I can't add anything to what I told the colonel," he said, intent on escaping their questions. "It followed the usual pattern."

"It strikes me that capturing a man who's made the Rock Island Railroad Company as much trouble as Buck Younger is anything but usual," Chauncey Dibbs declared emphatically. "It's a feather in your cap, Marshal. I can assure you there's four or five others in that gang the company would like to see behind the bars. I suppose they'll go after one of our trains next. We're open to it, all the way from Kingfisher north to the Kansas line. There ought to be a way of stopping it."

"What have you got to suggest?" Dick inquired, irked by the implied criticism. The sharpness of his tone was not lost on the freight agent.

"Don't get me wrong," he said, apologetically; "I wasn't trying to tell you how to handle things. What I was trying to say was that we know they'll strike again and that we ought to be able to find some way of getting ready for them. Putting armed guards on the trains would be expensive."

"That's been tried; it doesn't work out. You ought to be able to remember what happened following the holdup at Wharton, when the Santa Fe rounded up half a carload of gunmen and had them riding back and forth between Oklahoma City and Ponca. The Daltons no sooner heard about it than they let the Santa Fe know what they thought by sticking up another train for them."

"I suppose you're referring to the Carlin robbery," Dibbs said, with a supercilious laugh. He remembered it well enough and realized that its outcome made his suggestion ridiculous. "I know it was a fiasco. That wouldn't have been the case if the Santa Fe had managed things a little different. But everything seemed to go wrong."

Marr smiled thinly. "The only thing that went wrong was that as soon as the Daltons fired a shot, those gunmen were hugging the floor, looking for a hole to crawl into. They talked tough around Oklahoma City, but they didn't want any part of a scrap with that bunch. If you put guards on your trains, that's the kind you'll have to hire; they'll do a lot of swaggering, but they won't have any belly for facing the guns of as tough a gang as Morgan's put together."

He had had so much advice, most of it as absurd as Dibbs's chatter, heaped on him in his years as marshal that his patience had grown thin at having to listen to it. He hoped he had heard the last of it for this evening, but though the colonel, who knew how he felt, tried to turn the subject, the freight agent persisted.

"It's no great trick to figure out where bandits are going to hit you," was his cocksure assertion. "They pull their holdups only where they've got a quick and reasonably safe getaway open to them. Our water tank at the Turkey Creek crossing has always been a favorite spot with Morgan. There's been three robberies there and he's been in on every one of them. He may try it a fourth time."

Marr shrugged noncommittally, but Dibbs's prattling had suddenly begun to make sense to him. He was familiar with the lonely water tank at Turkey Creek, and he made a mental note to keep it in mind.

"Here's Belle, at last!" the colonel exclaimed. "I guess we can go in." The others moved into the dining-room; Marr waited for her.

"Pa told me you were here," she said. "I knew from the news we got this afternoon that we'd be seeing you soon. It's nice having you back at Woodhall Ranch again, Dick! I'm sorry I had to keep everyone waiting, but I just had to change," she continued, taking his arm.

He was so tall that she only came up to his chin. Gazing down at her fondly, he said, "You're always worth waiting for. You're particularly lovely tonight. I'd like to believe that my being here is responsible, but I'm afraid it's that new colt. I suppose he's going to be a champion."

She laughed, and it had a merry ring.

"It's foolish to predict anything for a foal that's only an hour old. He's a cute little shaver, Dick. Of course, he's all legs, but there's good blood in him, on both sides. Maybe he'll carry the Woodhall colors to victory one day."

Though she spent endless hours outdoors, her face and neck were not only untanned, but the sun and Oklahoma winds had not marred the flawless texture of her peach-white skin. Her copper-red hair set it off to perfection. In the strictest sense, she was not beautiful; she had her father's strong mouth, and it was too heavy for her delicately pointed chin. But her green eyes, alive, exciting and faintly reflecting the willfulness her father professed to see in her, were what a man saw and remembered.

At the table she refrained from asking Marr about the raid on Manatee. He knew it wasn't due to any lack of interest. He appreciated it all the more on that account. But Belle had sense and understanding, he told himself.

Oklahoma politics were buzzing again, and it provided the colonel and the others with a lively topic of debate as Black Ned and another servant moved around the table, serving an appetizing array of dishes and hot breads. The often heard, if homely, expression, "the colonel always sets a

51

heavy table," was as true tonight as usual. The food was excellent.

"If you could offer every voter a slice of this ranch-cured ham, Colonel, you Democrats would carry the election in a landslide," Skidmore declared, with a chuckle. "It's the best I've ever tasted!"

"We'll win without ham, Gil," Zach retorted. "Who are you going to get to vote for your man? A bunch of horse thieves?"

"Zach, if Gil gets every hoss thief in Oklahoma to vote for Hadley, he'll be elected by an overwhelming majority!" Henry Goss observed dryly.

Conversation in this vein couldn't last forever. Inevitably, someone said something about outlaws, and the bars were down.

"Calling a man an outlaw is just another way of saying he's a fool," Skidmore argued. "They all come to the same end eventually. They can't beat the law. I know Dick will agree to that." Marr nodded.

"I'll have to; the record speaks for itself. Where the outlaw is all wrong is in thinking that if he kills a marshal he's won free. But that isn't the case; if one of them dropped me tomorrow, there'd be another man stepping up to my place and the hunt would go on. I suppose outlaws have snuffed out half a hundred federal marshals in Oklahoma. It hasn't made the country safe for them. Quite the contrary. They know they're playing a losing game. Sooner or later, every last one of them dreams about making a stake and getting somewhere and going straight."

"But they never do it, Marr," said Chauncey Dibbs.

"No, they don't. The law has always got too many grudges against them."

"I don't believe that's the only reason, Dick," Belle remarked. "They've got used to that way of life—the thrills and excitement and danger of it. I can see how that would mean something to a man. I know it would mean something to me—the wild dash into a town to rob a bank, death riding at your elbow, and then the thrill of cowing everyone in sight just because you're Joe Doakes, the famous outlaw. The quick getaway then, and the long ride through hostile country to your hide-out! It would appeal to any man with imagination."

"Good Christopher, Belle, you sound as though you meant it!" old Zach snorted fiercely.

"I rather think I do," she said banteringly. "You see how lucky you are, Pa, that I'm a woman— and you always saying I should have been born a boy."

Taylor and Henry Goss laughed uproariously, and the latter said, "She's got you, Zach! You've been sayin' it for years!"

Marr gazed at Belle with an obscure interest and did not join in the merriment at the colonel's expense. As well as he knew her, it had given him a start to hear her speaking in that vein, her green eyes cold and reckless for a moment. He told himself there was no reason for surprise; she had been raised like a man and thought like one. He was so absorbed with his thinking that he was only vaguely aware of footsteps crossing the gallery. He turned his head, however, when he heard someone stop at the bench and deposit his gun. The next moment a man appeared in the entrance to the dining-room. Around the table tongues were stilled instantly. The marshal put down his knife carefully; the others froze in stiff, uncomfortable positions, Chauncey Dibbs with his fork half raised to his mouth; for the man who stood there was Britt Morgan, a smile on his intelligent, rather handsome face, his hair, black as a raven's wing and inclined to be curly about the ears, glinting in the lamplight.

He bowed to Belle and addressed himself to her father.

"May I invite myself to supper, Colonel?" he inquired with an assurance that completely ignored the fact that at that moment every peace officer in western Oklahoma was hunting him.

"Yes, sit down!" Zach jerked out.

Morgan approached the table, his blue eyes traveling from Belle to Marr and back to Belle. He sat down opposite Dick. "This seems to be a repetition of what happened to Uncle Ben Small

54

here at Woodhall Ranch when he was out looking for Joe Leclair," he said easily. "I never thought it would happen to me."

"It hasn't," Marr said coolly. "There was surprise on both sides that evening."

Morgan shrugged. "I hope that isn't the only difference. Uncle Ben caught up with Leclair two hours after they left here. I hope my luck runs a little better."

Chapter Four:
OUTWITTED

MARR REFUSED TO BELIEVE for a moment that Britt Morgan had presented himself at Woodhall Ranch out of bravado, or that he had weighed the risk he ran and concluded it was worth the gamble, hoping a bold move of this sort would advertise his fearlessness and pay future dividends. The marshal knew a far more urgent reason was responsible for Britt's presence, and that it undoubtedly concerned the wounded Buck Younger.

It left Marr with several surmises, and he canvassed each of them thoroughly in his mind. He could see how Morgan could have sent his men on across the Cimarron and turned south in the direction of the town of Woodhall with an extra horse to wait for Lem Shoup to bring Younger out to him after Wasson had patched him up. Morgan was well known in town, and the wisdom of not showing his face there was apparent. It was possible that he was unaware that Buck had been taken into custody.

Dick dismissed that thought promptly. The road between the ranch and the town was the most likely spot for Morgan to have waited for Shoup's wagon.

He had posted himself somewhere along the road and saw me pass, ran Marr's thoughts as he sat there, his face expressionless. *He knew he'd find me here when he walked in. Seeing I was in the neighborhood, especially alone, would have made him suspicious in a second.*

"I hadn't expected to sit down to such a spread as this," the bandit leader said lightly as Black Ned served him. "In fact, I had rather expected to miss my supper this evening."

Dick knew Morgan had had time enough to slip into town and learn how things stood. He was sure the danger of it wouldn't have held the man back, once the suspicion that Younger was a prisoner had taken possession of him. *He knows we've got Buck,* Marr told himself, picturing the scene at the depot. By now Huck and Lafe surely had Younger in the baggage room. *Showing up here and offering himself as a bait was a clever move!*

The game was not hard to fathom. Britt knew he was an even more important catch than Younger, and that when he pulled away from Woodhall Ranch the marshal could hardly resist the impulse to follow him. He was willing to take his chances on that if he could make Marr miss the night train south. To make sure that would happen, he would stall around until a few minutes before traintime before he made his dash. That Isbell and Roberts would start for Guthrie without Marr was very unlikely. That was the trick—to make them hold

Buck in the depot overnight. If Morgan could do that, he could be back before dawn with strength enough to stand a reasonable chance of taking the prisoner away from the marshals.

The longer Dick mulled it over the more ingenious the scheme appeared. But the old adage of the bird in hand being worth twice as much as the bird in the bush seemed to give him his answer. He'd play along with Morgan to a certain point, but he had Younger, and didn't propose to lose him.

It occurred to Marr that his logic might be wrong from first to last. Possibly the whole gang had witnessed the stopping of the wagon from a distance and had turned south with Morgan and were even then lying out within a few hundred yards of the depot. He found it hard to believe.

Morgan must have come down alone, he argued to himself. *If he had his gang with him he wouldn't have found it necessary to come in to the ranch.*

But doubt continued to gnaw at him. As for Britt, he seemed perfectly at ease. He had a gentlemanly air that was undeniable. The others had found their tongues, and when the conversation touched anything on which he had an opinion or knowledge, he expressed himself with an ingratiating degree of humility. He ate sparingly, and his manners were excellent.

Marr sensed Belle's interest in the man. Several times he thought he caught her studying him.

Whenever Morgan addressed her it was with a courtesy that robbed it of any offense. And yet Marr resented it. It was not what the bandit leader said half so much as his suavity and quiet swagger that irked him. He was glad when supper was finished.

The colonel got up heavily and stood waiting, expecting Morgan to thank him for his hospitality and take his departure. If the outlaw's horse was standing at the hitchrack, it was the only one there. It would take five to six minutes to bring a saddled animal up from the corral or barn. With such a start there would be little chance of overhauling him, the colonel felt.

Britt was not ready to leave, however, and old Zach was surprised to hear him say to Belle, "I saw your piano, Miss Woodhall. If you'll accompany me, I'll pay for my supper with a song."

The colonel scowled at the effrontery of it and expected Belle to put the man in his place. To his amazement, she met the suggestion with a smile. "I'm a poor accompanist, Mr. Morgan, but you may be able to follow me."

They went to the piano. In a strained silence that would have deterred most singers, Morgan lifted his baritone voice in the sad, sweet strains of "Come Where My Love Lies Dreaming." Only Belle applauded. With little urging from her, he continued with "Old Dog Tray" and several other sentimental ballads. Belle asked Marr to join in.

"No," he said stiffly, "I'm afraid the effect wouldn't be harmonious."

She knew he was annoyed with her, and with feminine perversity she begged Morgan to sing "Juanita," knowing Dick was particularly fond of the song. For good measure, she sang the chorus, her voice blending pleasantly with Britt's.

Marr turned away, his mouth hard. Through the open window he could see the cluster of lights that was the town. The train would be due in another 40 minutes. Morgan was drawing it almost too fine, he thought, hanging on like this.

I've got to allow myself five minutes to walk back to the depot, he mused soberly, damning the luck that had led him to have Rufe Perry's bronc put up, when the animal could just as well have remained at the rack until he was ready to leave.

As he stood there, brooding, a puff of sound reached his ears. He knew it was a shot, and it was followed by a sharp fusillade from half a dozen guns. The shooting came from town. Zach and the others heard it too. They rushed out on the gallery with him.

"That's shooting enough to spell trouble!" the colonel rapped, glancing at Marr.

At the piano Morgan's eyes sought Belle's. Something ran between them that held a deep understanding.

"I'm going," he murmured. "Play louder!"

She nodded, and her glance followed him as he stepped through a side window and disappeared into the night, He had left his horse on that side of the yard. A moment later the swift beating of shod hoofs rang out.

Marr popped into the room, Zach at his elbow.

"He's gone!" the colonel roared. "That was his horse we heard! Lord, Belle, stop banging that piano! Was that your idea of helping him to get out of the house without Dick hearing him?"

"How did he leave the room, Belle?" Marr asked, holding himself in.

"By the window behind me. I'm glad he got away—glad for his sake and yours, Dick!"

"That's fine talk, wasting your sympathy on that blackleg!" her father burst out violently. Belle's eyes flashed.

"I thought we were neutral here, Pa."

"Huh! There's a limit to my neutrality! I'm damned if I'll have that bandit shining up to you! I'll have a horse brought up for you, Dick!"

"Don't bother, Colonel," Marr answered, buckling on his gun belt. "I'll get there quicker if I run."

He hurried across the gallery and down the steps. The drumming of hoofs had faded to a whisper. In the direction of town the night was quiet again. It seemed to indicate that the issue there had been decided.

"Where did I go wrong?" he asked himself

repeatedly as his long legs carried him over the road.

He realized he was leaping to conclusions; a burst of gunfire didn't necessarily mean that Huck and Lafe had run into trouble. He was able to extract little or no hope from that possibility. There was a feeling in him, amounting almost to conviction, that this night's business had come to a disastrous end.

If a gun had flamed redly at his head, as he raced along, the deep dust muffling the thudding of his boots, it would not have surprised him. In a way, he would have welcomed it as proof that Morgan's men were still in the vicinity and had not been able to surprise his deputies. He was no longer of the opinion that Britt had ridden south alone.

"He had a man with him!" he muttered through clenched teeth. "He sent him up the river for help the minute he learned we had tripped Younger! That's where I made my mistake—never giving it a thought!"

His jaws clamped together tighter than ever when he caught sight of the depot. It was in darkness, not a light showing even in the agent's office. Lights burned in the windows of the stores across the street. They cast a faint radiance over the depot platform. When Marr turned off the road and started across the tracks, the store lamps outlined him. His foot had no more than touched the platform when a shot racketed out of the depot and carried away his hat. He flung himself to the planks and rolled up against the tiny building.

"Huck! Lafe!" he yelled. "Where are you?"

A burst of startled profanity in Huck Isbell's familiar voice answered him.

"Dick—is that you I was shootin' at?"

"Yeh! Where are you?"

"We're forted up here in the agent's office! We figgered you was one of the Morgans!"

The marshal got to his feet and ran into the baggage room. There was no one there. On the other side of the door he could hear a desk and chairs being pushed aside. A moment later Huck flung the door open. In the darkness Marr saw his deputies and a third man, Jeff Bannister, the agent.

"What happened?" he demanded without waiting to catch his breath.

"We got jumped as neat as you please!" little Lafe growled. "They took Younger away from us!"

"But how?" Marr rapped. "I know better than to think they caught you napping."

"Dick, they came at us two ways," Huck explained. "A couple of 'em popped in through that door facin' the tracks, shootin' as they came. A second later the rest of 'em dashes in through the door on the other side, where the wagons git loaded. We had Buck stretched out on a baggage truck. The first thing they done was to run the truck outside. Frank Cherry shot the lights out, and we had a hell of a go of it in here, dodgin' behind trunks and boxes and tryin' to git in a shot. I didn't see Morgan, but all the rest of 'em was in here."

"By cripes, we'll be the laughin' stock of the country over this!" Lafe groaned. "All we did was to git Buck fixed up for 'em!"

"We'll have the last laugh," Dick declared thinly. "Morgan walked in to supper at the ranch; that's why you didn't see him. He didn't bust away till we heard the shooting."

"By grab, you should have collared the dirty pup, and to hell with old Zach and his neutrality!"

"I couldn't do that, Lafe. What I should have done was to get back to you boys as soon as he showed up. I tried to figure out his play. I thought I had the answer; I was wrong. It was hoping for too much to expect any help from across the street."

"It ain't likely anybody knew what was happenin'—just a lot of shootin'," Bannister, the agent, interjected. "It was all over in four, five minutes. Is it all right for me to light the lamps?"

"Go ahead," Dick told him. "They got what they came for; they won't be back tonight." He dropped into a chair, shaking his head disgustedly. "The moment I saw Morgan I knew an attempt was going to be made to take Younger out of our hands. I didn't believe it would come before morning; I thought Britt was stalling around to make me miss the train."

He had more to say about what had passed through his mind at the ranch. Huck and Lafe had no fault to find with the conclusions he had reached.

"You got no reason to blame yourself," Isbell insisted. "If it had been me, I'd have figgered out his play jest the same way as you did."

"He had Cherry or Link Mulvey with him and had to give whoever it was time enough to git back with the rest of his wolves!" Little Lafe wagged his red head angrily. "It's easy enough to sit here and see the mistakes! But that's hindsight, and it ain't worth a damn! I don't know how you boys feel about it, but I got a personal score against that bunch now. I'll see the lot of 'em in hell before I'm finished!"

Bannister took a message off the wire. "That's Number Four," he said. "She's on time. Just pulled out of Wahuska."

He jerked out of his chair nervously as someone walked into the waiting-room. It was an elderly woman, alone. She came up to the ticket window.

"There ain't no more spunk in men these days than there is in a jack rabbit!" she exclaimed in a thin, caustic voice. "Half a dozen of 'em gathered in Simmons's store with their rifles and afraid to stick their noses outside! Told me there'd bin shootin' here at the depot an' I better not risk comin' over till they knew what had happened. I'm goin' to Kingfisher tonight, and I ain't missin' the train on account of some shootin'!"

Marr smiled to himself at the old woman's grit.

"Don't matter whether we take the train or not now," Huck remarked unhappily. "No use for us to git to Guthrie."

"We'll take Number Four," said Marr. "Our business with the Morgans won't be settled tomorrow or the next day, but it will be settled! We'll go to Guthrie and get organized and plan our campaign. I agree with Lafe that we've got a personal score against that bunch now. Robbing banks and trains is one thing; making us look foolish is something else, and I don't seem to have the humor to appreciate the joke!"

Chapter Five:
AN ALTERED DECISION

UNCLE BEN SMALL, still hale and hearty at 65, hurried to Guthrie to confer with Marr. He had looked so much trouble in the eye in his time that the storm of criticism with which the newspapers had greeted the robbery at Manatee and the emergence of still another gang of outlaws to plunder and terrorize Oklahoma did not rest too heavily on him.

"They're after my scalp, Dick," he declared in his matter-of-fact way, as they sat together in Marr's office in the federal jail. "Some of them are saying I'm falling down, getting too old for my job. The *Tribune* gives me a pat on the back for past performances and then hands me both barrels, saying I'm depending too much on my deputies and their field marshals." He leaned back in his chair and laughed mirthlessly. "I guess we'll manage to weather the storm! After we smashed the Doolin gang, these same newspaper fellows who are hammering us now were shouting that organized outlawry was a thing of the past in Oklahoma. I never encouraged that idea; I was sure someone like Morgan would draw all the loose ends together and have another last try at the game. It would have taken the sting out of things if you'd been able to hang on to Younger, Dick."

Marr nodded. "It's a bitter pill for me to swallow, Uncle Ben. It was my fault he got away."

He gave the old man hunter a detailed account of what had happened at Woodhall Ranch and the depot. Uncle Ben listened without comment. At the end he sat there twiddling his fingers absent-mindedly for a moment or two. "You can call it your fault if you want to," he said, his eyes keen and snapping as he looked up. "I see it a different way. If Zach Woodhall wasn't the biggest damned fool in seven states, you could have nailed Morgan and hung on to Younger, too!" He snorted disgustedly. "Zach's ideas were all right fifteen years ago; they're just nonsense today! But don't let it get you down, Dick. I've made bigger mistakes and managed to come out on top. Have you made any plans?"

"I'm going to ship our horses and riding gear up to Woodhall and make my headquarters there. That'll put us astraddle of the Rock Island. The Santa Fe will be only twenty-eight miles east of us. If we try to stop Morgan from slipping through to knock off a bank somewhere, we'll be chasing him for the rest of our lives. It'll be a different story when he goes after a train. Sooner or later we'll surprise him."

"That's right; watch the railroads," Uncle Ben agreed. "You'll need more men, Dick. I'll send Jim Bryan and Pat Curry up to you tomorrow. I'm not going to tell you how to play your hand; you know what's required as well as I do. Just don't take any unnecessary chances. Morgan's got some wild men riding with him. They're killers. If you get to close quarters with them, don't bother trying to take them alive. Are you going to try to buy any information?" Marr shook his head.

"You can't rely on it, Uncle Ben. But I've got some contacts; news will be sifting through to me. Ri Carver is my best bet. If he picks up anything he thinks I ought to know, he'll let me hear from him."

"Is he home?" the old marshal inquired.

"No, he pulled out of Bowie about three weeks ago. He follows the Cimarron all the way out to the Ratons on his spring trip. He must be heading back across No Man's Land by now."

Darius "Doc" Carver and his traveling drugstore had been disappearing into the prairie wilderness west of the river at regular intervals for many years. His familiar covered wagon was a welcome sight at the lonely dugouts and ranches. He went where he pleased and was never molested. Though he was neither doctor nor dentist, he often obliged in both roles, delivering babies and pulling teeth with satisfactory results to his patients. He never betrayed a confidence, but he kept his eyes and ears open, and if a man with a criminal record sat down at Carver's campfire he was sure to be given a sizzling lecture against lawlessness.

"Ri's a good man," Uncle Ben observed. "It may be some time before you hear from him. It's my guess that Morgan will lay low till some of the hue and cry dies down, and then raid into Kansas, for a change."

They talked for an hour and found themselves in complete agreement. Uncle Ben had often said that when he stepped down he wanted Marr to take his place.

"Don't let your patience wear thin," he cautioned, as he was leaving. "I'll be in touch with you. When you see Zach, give him hell for me!"

Twenty-four hours later Marr and his field marshals were established in the miserable little hotel at Woodhall. His new men, Bryan and Curry, had proved their mettle on numerous occasions, and he congratulated himself on having them with him.

Colonel Woodhall came over, protesting that they should have made the ranch their head-quarters.

"You'd have been comfortable, Dick. There isn't a decent bed in this place."

"I don't expect to have much use for a bed for the next week or two," Marr answered. "I've got some traveling to do. While I'm gone, I want my men where I can reach them by wire in a hurry."

"Well, you will drop over when you get the chance?"

"Not if it means taking off my guns, Colonel."

"You'll never have to do that on my account— not after what happened night before last!" old Zach exclaimed violently. "There won't be any more guns placed on the bench that's stood at my door for years; I busted it to kindling yesterday morning and flung it into the fire! Times have changed, and I should have realized it a long while back!"

Marr smiled. "I'm glad you've come around to seeing it that way. How is Belle?"

"I don't know! We ain't speaking. I gave her a dressing down for carrying on the way she did with Morgan. She fought back and we had a big row. She had a horse saddled and was away from the house most of yesterday and again today."

Dick took it lightly. "You better try to patch things up, Colonel," he advised. "You can't get anywhere with Belle by using the whip."

He went up to Wahuska that afternoon. It was the first of many stops for him. The next day he had got as far north as Enid, after conferring with local peace officers along the way. There, he took the Southwestern to Blackwell and began moving south along the Santa Fe. He left the railroad at Orlando and hired a rig to drive him over to Manatee, where he found Rufe Perry patrolling the street. They walked back to Rufe's little office.

"I've been making a swing around to the towns north of you," Marr told him.

"So I heard," Rufe said. "I reckon Enid is the only town up there that feels safe. What have you been tellin' the boys?"

"To get three or four good men lined up, Rufe, and pick out a spot from which they can keep the bank covered. Most of these towns have only one bank. Being ready for a raid and throwing some lead at the right time will accomplish more than organizing a dozen posses and chasing across country after your bandits."

"I agree with every word of that!" was Rufe's response. "I figger if I had been up there on the hotel roof the afternoon the Morgans was in, I could have stopped 'em. Is there any news of 'em leakin' through?"

"Just a rumor that they were seen heading toward the Salt Fork two days ago."

"Yeh?" Rufe queried with sudden interest. "If they're that far north, sounds like they had Kansas on their minds. They may find them Kansas sheriffs waitin' for 'em."

"I hope so, Rufe. At least, I've notified them."

Marr kept an eye on the clock as they talked. Anything concerning Buck Younger's capture and escape was by now a sore point with him, but Perry insisted on getting the details firsthand.

"That's a little different than I heard it," Rufe declared. "I'm glad to git it straight. I don't know whether it's occurred to you or not, Dick, but it looks queer to me how Morgan should know his way around Woodhall Ranch like that. It almost makes me think he's been there before."

"What do you mean by that?" Marr asked, his tone sharper than he realized. "You certainly don't believe the colonel is holding back anything, do you?"

"No, no chance of that! But I'll bet my shirt there's someone there who's sayin' less than he knows! I see you watchin' the clock. You takin' the train south?"

"As far as Bowie Junction. It'll put me in Woodhall tonight. I've been gone ten days; I'm a little anxious to get back."

Rufe grabbed his hat. "We better be movin'," he said. "I'll walk down with you."

The train rolled in almost as soon as they reached the depot. Dad Finney, the conductor, called a greeting to Marr and hurried to the agent's window for his orders.

"Young Bill Woodhall seems to be goin' from bad to worse," Rufe remarked, apparently apropos of nothing at all. "He talks a lot when he's drunk, and that seems to be most of the time."

All this indirection did not fool Dick.

"So it's Bill you suspect," he declared bluntly.

Rufe scowled and said, "It's easy to suspect a fool! You think it over!"

Marr did little else on the ride to Bowie. Despite

73

his feeling that Perry's suggestion was without merit, he was compelled to admit, for all his skepticism, that the way Morgan and his men had moved back and forth across the colonel's range that day and early evening, without being seen, indicated a certain familiarity with the ranch. The dispatch with which he had brought up his gang for the attack on the depot was further proof of it.

Though it was a disturbing admission, Marr could find no reason for connecting young Bill Woodhall with it. He found it much easier to believe that some of the ranch crew had been bribed.

Two days after Dick's return to Woodhall, Huck Isbell came running from the depot in the middle of the afternoon. "Dick, the news has jest come through that the Morgans rode into Sumner, Kansas, at noon!" he burst out excitedly.

"How much did they get?" Marr snapped.

"Not a cent! They ran into gunfire before they got off their hosses! They was stopped cold! When they pulled out, they left one deputy sheriff dead and a couple more badly wounded."

"Kansas don't pay!" little Lafe chuckled grimly. "Coffeyville finished the Daltons, and the Doolins got smacked at Cimarron City. I figgered Morgan would be too smart to try it."

"Uncle Ben didn't," said Marr. "He called the turn. This may give us the break we've been asking for. Morgan will certainly come down across the salt flats and through the Galena Hills before he crosses the Cimarron. We can be there, waiting for them. They'll be smart enough not to crowd their horses too much. It'll be an hour or two after sunrise before they see the river. I'll go over to the depot now and have Bannister wire Kingfisher to have an extra baggage car put on Number Two for our horses. We'll leave the train at Waukomis and hit our saddles. We'll be where we're going by midnight."

At the depot he waited until word came back from Kingfisher that the car he had requested would be put on the train. It left him better than two hours to wait, and with time to spare, he rode over to the ranch.

Belle stepped out on the gallery as he got down. He was a little surprised to see her, for she was not usually in the house at this time of the day. He had seen her for a few minutes since getting back. In some indefinable way she had seemed changed, preoccupied. She and her father were still at odds, and he put it down to that.

"Come up and sit down, Dick," she urged, studying him carefully without seeming to. "I'll have Ned fetch you a drink. You look to me like a man who might have something on his mind," she added, with a semblance of her old gaiety. "I hope you're not going to tell me the Morgans have broken loose again."

"Sumner, Belle," he replied. "They rode in about

noon to knock off the bank and got turned back. They killed one man and badly wounded a couple more."

The pulse in her left cheek began to beat madly.

"I don't like to hear that," she said tensely and looked away. "Did—the Morgans lose anyone?"

Marr failed to realize what the question cost her.

"Apparently not," he said. "But they're not out of it yet. If I have any luck, Sumner will be their last raid. I'm going alter them, Belle, and I don't see how I can miss them."

"I hope you're right, Dick," she answered guilelessly.

She rang for old Ned. Marr said a julep would please him. He asked about the colonel.

"Pa's down at the lower corral," Belle told him, with a lightness she was far from feeling. "The boys are getting some calves ready to ship."

Marr's confidence in her was such that he never suspected the adroitness with which she got him to unfold his plans.

"I don't know," she murmured skeptically. "Galena Crossing may be the place to look for them. If this were late July or August, I think I would agree with you. But the river is still high, Dick; there'll be a lot of water at the Galena Crossing. I know if I were Britt Morgan I wouldn't cross there, not when I could turn west about two miles to Burdette's Ford and be sure I wouldn't have any trouble. But don't let me sway you."

Marr laughed at her sudden seriousness.

"I'm glad you're not Britt Morgan," he said. "But there's something to what you say, Belle. They could skirt the Galena Hills and make Burdette's Ford without adding anything to the distance to the river."

"There's good cover coming down to the ford from the north. That's an advantage they're not apt to overlook." She was far too clever to urge her argument too strongly, though it was nothing short of a matter of life and death for Britt. Deliberately, she turned the conversation to other things half a dozen times as Marr sipped the julep Ned had brought out. But she always managed to revert to the subject of Burdette's Ford. She could see that he was wavering, undecided.

"I don't want you to be left holding an empty bag a second time, Dick," she said, with deceiving innocence. "If you knew where they crossed on their way north, there wouldn't be much doubt of where to look for them tomorrow morning."

"No, there wouldn't," he admitted.

"I'd have a look at the ford if I were you. A good tracker like Lafe Roberts would be able to tell you if they passed there. The story must still be there in the mud."

Marr slapped his knee, his decision reached. Belle knew she had won.

"There's a lot of hard sense in you, Belle," he said admiringly. "We'll have to pass Galena Crossing to reach the ford. It'll be late, but the moon will be bright tonight. If we don't find any sign there, we'll go on to Burdette's Ford." He caught her hand and pressed it affectionately. "I wish I could bring all my problems to you. You know I've felt that way for a long time, Belle."

"I know, Dick," she murmured, turning her head so that he might not see the harried look in her eyes. "I've often wished things were different, and never so much as now."

"What makes you say that?" he asked, regarding her fondly. She shook her head.

"You wouldn't understand. You're decent and honorable, Dick; I don't want to hurt you. But Pa's right about me; I'm selfish and willful and seven kinds of a fool. I—I hope you'll never turn against me—no matter what I do."

His fingers tightened on her hand. "I'll always love you, Belle," he said, his heart in his eyes. "Always. There'll never be anyone else for me."

The simple declaration touched her, and she had to bite back her emotion. "Please, Dick, don't say any more," she begged, a suspicious quaver in her usually steady voice. The nervous tension she had been under all day was becoming more than she could bear.

Her brother Bill strolled out on the gallery. They had never been good friends, but, for once, she was glad to see him. He gave Marr and her a smirking, sidelong glance as he went down the steps. He looked what he was, lazy, dissolute.

"My sweet and loving little sister!" he mocked.

Here was escape for Belle, and she leaped to embrace it. "Damn you, Bill, keep a civil tongue in your mouth! I'll use a whip on you if you don't!"

He gave her an impudent grin. "You can't take it, can you? But you've always got your nose in my business. Maybe I can do a little blabbing—"

"Bill, I warned you!" she cried, mingled fear and anger whitening her cheeks. A coiled stock whip caught her eye. She plucked it off the shelf where it lay and straightened it out behind her on the gallery floor. Bill Woodhall had seen her use a sixteen-foot whip many times. With its leaden popper, it was a deadly weapon. He knew she wouldn't hesitate to use it on him.

Dick was used to their quarreling and didn't take it seriously, though he had seldom seen Belle so angry.

"Don't blow up," Bill said placatingly. "I was just having a little fun with you!"

"All right!" Belle exclaimed, her green eyes as menacing as ever. "Just remember when you're speaking to me you're not talking to one of your Guthrie strumpets!"

Bill hung on, trying to find a fitting retort. But the colonel came around the corner, and that ended it. Belle pulled herself together quickly and tried to recover her lost dignity. "I'm sorry I let myself go like that, Dick," she said apologetically. "Bill always infuriates me."

"I thought you gave a good account of yourself," Marr said, laughingly, and then, "I'll let you know how things go."

"Do! I'll be anxious to know."

Night overtook Marr and his four men soon after they rode west from Waukomis. In the early evening they crossed the upper stretch of Turkey Creek. They had several small crossroads towns ahead of them. They gave them a wide berth. Most of this country was still raw land, the roads just meandering trails across the prairie.

A full moon made the night bright. They moved along freely, and it lacked an hour of midnight when Lafe Roberts, with the sureness of a homing pigeon, led them to the Galena crossing of the Cimarron.

"The river isn't as high as I thought it might be," Marr remarked. He had told the others of his changed plans.

"She's high," said Lafe. "You boys hold back and let me have a look down there."

He studied the ground for some time before he walked back to where they waited.

"Don't look like anybody had crossed here this spring," he announced. "Plenty tracks, but they was made last fall. You want Huck or someone else to have a look, Dick?"

"No, you wouldn't be wrong about anything like that. We'll go on to the ford."

It did not take them long to cover the several miles to the Burdette crossing. A long, gentle slope led down to the river. They approached it with increased caution. The cover Belle had mentioned was there, willow brakes and a tangle of wild oak and blackjack scrub.

"A nice spot for a bushwhacking party," Jim Bryan remarked warily. He was seeing it for the first time. "If this is where we're going to meet them, we'll have them dead to rights when they ride down this slope."

There were no lurking foes in the trees. Lafe went down to the river's edge as he had done at the other crossing; it was only a minute before he called back that he had found fresh tracks. Dick joined him.

"How old are they, Lafe?"

"Three, four days. There's a bunch of 'em. Take six, seven hosses to cut the ground up like this. Reckon it's a shore bet the Morgans crossed here."

"There wouldn't seem to be any doubt of it," the marshal agreed. "As Jim just said, we've got everything in our favor. We'll put our broncs back in the trees and get set. I expect we'll have a long wait. It may get a little chilly before morning."

They hid the horses and took up a position that commanded the slope and the ford.

"Let's git it straight," Huck growled. "How we goin' to handle 'em when they show up?"

"We'll let them come on till they're abreast of us," Marr told him. "We'll have them covered all the while. I'll give them a call to throw up their hands."

"They'll never do it!" Lafe insisted.

"I don't suppose they will. They'll most surely reach for their guns. When they do, we'll open up on them."

By three o'clock the air was so cold along the river bottom that it set Huck's teeth to chattering.

"Yo're goin' like a thrashin' machine!" Lafe complained. "What's the matter with you?"

"It's that dang Mizzoura ague! Got it in my bones. I'll shore be glad to see that sun peepin' over the Galena Hills!"

A coyote trotted down the slope, coming in for water, and got their scent. He bounded away, and from a distant ridge made the night hideous with his barking.

Dawn was a long time coming, it seemed. But at last the sky began to brighten; the mist started rising from the bottoms, and the chill worked out of the air.

"We can expect them any time now," Dick observed soberly. The others nodded, tension building up in them. At one time or another each had shot it out with some member of the gang Morgan had riding with him. Mulvey and Cherry and Buck Younger, if he chanced to be with them, and all the rest were a hard-bitten crew, fearless in the face of gunfire. Getting the jump on them didn't mean they wouldn't fight as long as they could squeeze a trigger.

Marr awaited their coming with quiet confidence. To have the issue decided here was better than he had dared to hope. He had seen himself spending the summer and fall hunting them down.

The sun climbed higher, and the morning turned warm and balmy. He looked at his watch.

"After six," he said. "They're late. They must be carrying some wounded men with them."

Seven o'clock came, and doubts began to assail him. They grew by the minute. Lafe and Huck were equally pessimistic.

"Looks like we had our trouble for nuthin'!" the latter growled.

"They had to come down across the salt flats," Marr argued. "There was no other way."

"I got to agree with that," Huck got out glumly. "But they didn't have to head for this ford. They could have got across at Galena. Suppose I ride over there and have a look."

Dick shook his head firmly. "We'll stick it out a while longer. I still believe we'll see them."

He was only voicing a fading hope. By eight o'clock he knew it was next to useless to wait there any longer. Even so, he decided to hang on while Isbell rode back to Galena Crossing. The latter had been gone not more than 40 minutes, when he came pounding back. He had found bountiful evidence that Britt had led his men across the river at that point.

"It's as plain as print, Dick! While we was squattin' here, they was gittin' acrost!"

Marr received the news with a grim face. He didn't trust himself to speak for a minute.

"You had the right hunch in the first place, Dick. What made you change yore mind?" Lafe demanded, bitter disappointment racking him.

Marr's temper snapped. "Because I was convinced our chances were better here!" was his angry answer, his face hard and flat. "Does that answer you?" he whipped out, thinking of Belle.

Chapter Six:
BELLE SHOWS HER HAND

THOUGH IT MEANT a stern chase, with the advantage all with Morgan, Marr ordered his men across the Cimarron. The sober, ice-cold judgment that had served him so well in the past told him that if there was to be any surprise now it would be of Britt's making.

Huck and the others realized as well as he that any clump of trees or high brush might suddenly burst into flame. But there was little time to be cautious; they had to ride or have no chance at all of overtaking their quarry.

They spread out in a thin line as they advanced, knowing it would be fatal to run into an ambush if they were bunched together. Lafe rode in the lead, following the bandits' trail with little difficulty. Not a shot broke the morning stillness. The trail continued to stretch away ahead of them; they saw no one. The wind stiffened and stirred the brush and trees; nothing else moved.

"I can see where this is takin' us!" Lafe called to Marr. "It's headin' straight for the North Fork of the Canadian! If they got any reason to suspect we're behind 'em, they'll make a stand there or shake us off!"

Another eight miles brought them to the tree-choked bottoms of the North Fork. They advanced with drawn guns, but there was no one there to challenge them. The trail that had been so easy to follow all the way down from the Cimarron seemed to fade into thin air. Lafe tried in vain to pick it up.

"Reckon that stops us," Huck grumbled. "We gave it a good try, if that helps any!"

Marr had to concede defeat. Reluctantly he gave the word to turn east. Late that afternoon they rode their jaded horses into Woodhall. They were as weary as their mounts; and they had gone hungry since leaving Waukomis the previous evening.

"If a good meal can be squeezed out of this joint, it better show up on the table this evenin'!" little Lafe grumbled as he climbed the stairs with Marr. "I reckon you'll be goin' over to the ranch for supper."

"No, I'm going to stretch out for an hour. Wake me up when you're ready to go down."

Some of the colonel's punchers were in town. They heard that the marshals had returned, and they carried the news to the ranch. Half an hour later Dick found Lafe bending over him, shaking him awake.

"Suppertime already?" he asked sleepily. "Seems like I just closed my eyes."

"Miss Belle's downstairs. She's waitin' outside in a rig for you. I didn't tell her you was sleepin'; I figgered you'd want to see her."

Marr nodded. "Say I'll be down in a couple minutes, Lafe."

Since early morning he had been telling himself that he couldn't hold Belle responsible for his failure. He had been swayed by her advice, but only because he had found it logical and well reasoned.

It could have been the other way around just as easy as not, he thought, dousing his face in a basin of cold water. *I'm kicking myself over the way things turned out, but I'd have felt even worse if we had stuck it out at Galena and they had slipped across at Burdette's Ford.*

Belle steeled herself to meet him, and when he came up to her buggy her gay smile hid the anxiety that was tearing at her. "I just heard you were back, Dick. I hadn't expected you so soon. How did things go?"

"They didn't go my way at all," he confessed. "I don't want you to feel bad about it, Belle," he added hastily as he saw her straighten up.

He told her what had happened. Her white teeth bit deeply into her lower lip.

"I shouldn't have said anything," she murmured self-accusingly, even as a warm glow of relief stole through her. "I told you not to pay any attention to what I said. You'll never forgive me!"

"Nothing of the sort!" he assured her. "It was just rotten luck that we missed them. I know they went north by way of Burdette's. Morgan must have figured that they might have been seen, and if anybody was waiting for him on the way down, he'd cross them up by using Galena. It's a tough break, but he won't take all the tricks, Belle. I haven't mentioned our talk to anyone. It'll be better if it's just forgotten."

She felt she was on safe ground again, and after berating herself further, for her meddling, she asked him to ride home with her. Dick begged off, saying he would eat with his men and turn in for the night.

"Well, don't be a stranger," she said.

"I'll be over when I can," he promised.

He received several conflicting reports concerning the whereabouts of the Morgans in the days that followed. One, from a source that he had always found reliable, said Britt had been seen alone, a few miles west of Woodhall. He discussed it at length with Huck and the others. It was Lafe's opinion that Morgan had come in to size up some bank.

"He'd come alone on a job of that sort. I don't put no stock in the other stories we bin hearin'. That bunch ain't movin' too much. They're holed up somewheres between the Cimarron and the North Fork."

"I'm not so much interested in where they are as what their next move is going to be," Dick observed, glancing at the map on the wall. "I don't know what Britt's got his eye on this time, but he knows we're sitting here and that if he goes after anything east of Woodhall he'll find us between him and the river. Maybe that won't stop him; he may have a try at some place like Bowie or Orlando. I hope he does; we couldn't ask for anything better."

Uncle Ben arrived unexpectedly in Woodhall the following morning. What he had to say made it appear that hoisting another bank might not be the Morgans' next objective. There was to be a big shipment of money from a Kansas City bank coming down on Friday. The Rock Island would be carrying it, and the railroad company was concerned about its getting through safely.

"It'll be on Number Four, Dick. She goes through here about nine o'clock, doesn't she?"

"Nine-five if she's on time. She makes three stops between Woodhall and Kingfisher, counting the stop for water at the Turkey Creek tank."

"No telling where they may try to nail her," Uncle Ben declared with his customary bluntness. "There may be nothing to it; railroad officials scare awfully easy. Then, again, they may know what they're talking about. I've never been able to figure out how a bandit like Morgan could get wind of a shipment coming through, but both of us have seen it happen. I suppose somebody tips them off for a slice of the money. Anyway, I told the Rock Island you'd ride Number Four Friday night. You better board her up at Enid and go all the way through to El Reno. If you're stuck up, all the better."

"That'd suit me fine," Dick assured him. "If the Morgan gang climbs into that express car they'll find quite a reception waiting for them."

Marshal Ben nodded. "They likely have someone keeping cases on you. Get your men out of town without attracting too much attention."

"I'll send Bryan and Curry up to Enid on Thursday. Huck and Lafe can go Friday morning. I'll catch the afternoon train. Have you anything better to suggest?"

"No, that sounds okay. I'll see that the Rock Island will be looking for you at Enid. That's about all the business I've got on my mind. I'm going over to the ranch and spend an hour with Zach and sample some of his fried chicken. Will you come along, Dick?"

"No, Uncle Ben, I won't. I've got a sick horse on my hands—that big bay I've owned so long— and I want to see what I can do about it."

The old marshal nodded understandingly. "You run along, then. I won't come back. I'll just stay at the ranch till traintime and make it look as though I didn't come up with anything particular on my mind."

Isbell and the others received the news of promised action with undisguised relief. Sweating it out around Woodhall had begun to get on their nerves. All through Wednesday they talked of little else. Bryan and Curry pulled out for the north on Thursday, and Huck and Lafe followed the next morning, as Marr had planned.

It was quite the usual thing for Belle Woodhall to be seen in town, shopping or visiting. She not only happened to see Bryan and Curry take the train north, but when Isbell and Roberts walked over to the depot, she found an excuse for speaking to Jeff Bannister, the agent. She was in time to hear the two field marshals ask for tickets to Enid. That afternoon, when Marr started across the street to the railroad, she hailed him from her buggy, standing in front of Simmons's store.

"We're having wild turkey for supper, Dick. Won't you come over?"

Marr shook his head and laughed regretfully,

"I've got to miss it, Belle. And you know I'm fond of wild turkey! I'm taking the train."

"That's too bad," she protested. "Where are you off to this time?"

"Enid," he said, all unsuspicious. The north-bound train was in sight. "Save a slice of that turkey for me, Belle! I've got to run now. I'll be back in the morning!"

It was a simple matter for her to put the pieces of the puzzle together. A day or two ago Marshal Small had come to Woodhall; yesterday two of Marr's men had gone north; today Huck and Lafe had followed them, and now Dick himself was on his way to Enid. It was all she needed to know.

When she returned to the ranch, she had a horse saddled at once. No one asked where she rode, but supper was cold on the table by the time she got back. Number Four stood panting at the depot in Enid even then. In the combination baggage and express car Marr and his field marshals, rifles handy, were settling down for the night ride to El Reno.

The express messenger glanced up nervously from his desk, where he was finishing his Enid work. His green eyeshade gave his plump face a ghostly pallor. Marr dragged an old side-arm chair over to the desk.

"Have you ever run into a holdup?" he inquired.

"Twice, Marshal. Once at Turkey Creek, and the other time it was the Wharton robbery. Dan Scribner was riding express with me that night. Doolin yelled at him to drop his gun. He refused to do it, so they killed him. Morgan got him. I didn't get a scratch." He sighed heavily. "It makes me wonder about tonight; a man's luck don't hold good forever. You know the saying—three times and out."

"I don't believe there's any reason for you to be alarmed," Marr told him. "If we're stopped and you're called on to open up, roll the door back and get out of the way. Get rid of that forty-five you've got on your hip. You better do it right now; we'll take care of whatever fighting has to be done. I don't want any wild shooting in this car."

They felt the air hoses tighten as the engineer tested the brakes. A low toot of the whistle followed. A shiver ran down the length of the train, and Number Four was moving out of Enid. She gathered speed quickly. The express car began to rock and sway on its trucks.

"Who have we got in the cab tonight?" Lafe asked the messenger, as the cinders began to rain down on the roof.

"Pat Hanks."

Little Lafe nodded dubiously. "He's shore got her wide open!"

They struck a stretch of roadbed on which work had been done recently. A pall of red dust sucked down through the ventilators and sifted in through the doors and barred windows. The ceiling lamps shone through it feebly.

Waukomis was their first stop. Nobody found anything worth saying as the train roared through the night; but their memories ran back to another night when the old Doolin gang had swarmed over Number Four at Waukomis.

The whistle screeched and the engineer began to put on the air. The train lost speed quickly. Huck glanced at Marr.

"Waukomis," he muttered woodenly. "This could be it, Dick!"

"Yeh," the marshal agreed laconically. "We're ready, if it is."

Number Four discharged some passengers, took

on others going south; the express messenger delivered and received an assortment of packages; in the mail car, just behind, the clerk did the same. Nothing happened to break the peaceful routine of the operation.

It was the same at Ranger, Wetonka, and Wahuska.

"Be rich if it turned out to be Woodhall!" Pat Curry, who seldom had anything to say, observed with an ironic laugh.

Woodhall was just a flag stop for Number Four. The train slowed as it neared the little town and then gathered speed again. Marr and the others sat back, both relieved and disappointed.

"We're gittin' down purty far," said Lafe.

"Look out for the Turkey Creek tank," Dick advised, recalling what Chauncey Dibbs had said that night at Woodhall Ranch. "Morgan's always been lucky there."

There was a brief stop at Magoffin. The express messenger ran the door back a foot or two, and the local agent came running to receive several packages. The messenger closed the door with a bang. At half speed Number Four rumbled across the Turkey Creek bridge and ground to a stop at the water tank. The marshals tightened their grip on their rifles, expecting every second to bring the cracking of guns and the summons to open the door. In the trees along the creek bottom the cicadas and katydids continued their raucous singing uninterrupted, however. The fireman climbed over the coal and pulled down the spout; the rushing of water into the tender followed.

Huck cleared his throat, and the sound ran to the far corners of the car on the tense, charged air. The fireman clambered back to the cab. There was a sound of steam escaping from the exhaust valves. The wheels turned, and Number Four began to roll away.

"Dammit!" Lafe cursed. "That jest about settles it! Ain't a chance in a hundred now that we'll see anythin' of the Morgans tonight!"

"Aw, that's all right, Lafe," Huck declared sarcastically. "I'm shore the fathead who dreamed up this idea and ran to Uncle Ben with it won't forgit to send us a nice letter of thanks for the trouble we bin put to. Reckon we can relax."

Though Dick felt as they did, he said, "It's a little early to count Morgan out; we've still got some distance to go. Suppose we wait until we hit El Reno before we give ourselves another zero."

But Number Four clicked off the miles and made its scheduled stops without anything more exciting than a hotbox to break the monotony of its run.

In El Reno, Marr changed his mind about returning to Woodhall in the morning and went on to Oklahoma City. A case was coming to trial in the federal court at Guthrie in a day or two that necessitated his presence as a witness.

On Sunday, as he was about to enter the hotel for dinner, Bill Woodhall shuffled out, his step unsteady. Marr said hello and would have stepped inside, but Bill caught his arm.

"What you doing, brushing me off?" he demanded crossly. "I want to talk to you. When you going to get wise to yourself, Dick? Belle's making a fool of you!"

Marr's face whipped tight in a second.

"You're drunk, Bill, but that won't save you with me if you try to dirty Belle's name. I'll smack you down as sure as you're standing there!"

"Sucker!" young Woodhall sneered. "She's been riding up the river and meeting Morgan every few days! She knows all his plans! That's why she talked you into going to Burdette's Ford! She knew they were going to cross at Galena!"

Something snapped in Dick, and he grabbed Bill by the collar and cocked his arm to flatten him.

"Go ahead, knock me down!" Woodhall invited. "The old man says I'm the black sheep of the family. He's got a surprise coming to him! Who do you think tipped Morgan off that you and your men were in Enid, coming down on Number Four?"

Marr didn't wait for any more. A blinding rage, such as he had never known, gripped him. His fist flashed out and crashed into Bill's jaw, sending him crumpling to the sidewalk. All thought of dinner forgotten, he turned back to his office.

He called up all his faith in Belle to steady him. He told himself Bill was lying; that she couldn't have betrayed him. He refused to believe she had been trysting with Morgan these past weeks. But there was the fiasco at the ford; the failure of the gang to stop the train. He had told her he was going to Enid. How easily she could have learned that Huck and the others had gone up ahead of him! He knew he had to hurry back to Woodhall, if only for an hour. He had to see Belle! Nothing else mattered now!

There was only one train on Sundays that made connections at Kingfisher. He caught it, and it put him in Woodhall in the early evening. He started for the ranch on foot, at once.

Just what it was, he couldn't tell, but as he reached the rambling house he felt an air of tragedy, of brooding stillness hanging over it, as though something had happened that had crushed its heart and gay laughter and left only the walls and roof standing.

Never before had he walked up the gallery steps without someone coming out to greet him. He walked to the end of the gallery and glanced down at the bunkhouse. A number of the crew were gathered there, just sitting around and not indulging in their usual pranks.

Dick heard a step behind him. He turned and found old Ned standing there, despair written deep in his black face.

"Everything seems strange around here today, Ned," he got out anxiously. "Where's Miss Belle?"

The old man shook his head sadly. "She ain't here, Mist' Dick!"

Marr stiffened at the implication in the Negro's words and tone. "What do you mean—she isn't here?"

"She's lef' us." Ned's chin quivered with the misery that was in him. "She's runned off wid Britt Morgan. Sometime in the night she went. She lef' a letter fer de colonel. Miss Belle say dey got a preacher from Magoffin ter marry 'em."

Marr stood there, a stricken look on his lean face. So it was true, what Bill had said! Belle married to Britt Morgan! It was as though the stars had fallen out of the sky. He recalled her saying she hoped he would never turn against her no matter what she did. It was this she had meant!

He gazed at Ned. The old man was sniffling softly, tears running down his ebony cheeks. Somehow, they seemed close to each other, drawn together by a common bond, and the fact that their skins were of a different color did not matter.

"It's going to be hard for us, Ned; both of us love her."

"Yas suh, Mist' Dick. Don' seem like dere's any use tryin' ter go on. Ah seen dat chile grow up; dere was nebber anyone like her. She was de life and spirit dat was Woodhall. Ain't nothin' left yere now but an ole man and some memories."

Dick asked about Zach. Ned told him the colonel was sleeping. "Doctor Wasson bin yere 'mos' all day, Mist' Dick. He gib him sumpin' ter put him to sleep. Colonel, he nebber goin' ter amount ter nuthin' no moh. He ain' got even Mist' Bill ter lean on."

"You stick with him, Ned." Marr's voice was gruff and strange. He put his hand on the black man's shoulder. "He's going to need you more than ever now. I'll be back later."

His face was stony as he went down the steps and started walking. Halfway to town, he turned off the road and started across the prairie, walking faster. He felt he couldn't face Huck and Lafe and their questions tonight.

Chapter Seven:
"LET'S RIDE!"

HUCK AND LAFE LEARNED that Dick had been in Woodhall and had returned to Guthrie without seeing them. They understood why. They knew how to show the world a flinty face, but beneath their walrus hides there was as much feeling and sentiment as the average man possessed. Perhaps a little more.

"This was a crack in the face that he won't git over in a hurry," little Lafe proclaimed glumly, as he and Huck sat on the hotel porch one evening. "We can make it a little easier by keepin' our mouths shut about it when he gits back."

"Who's thinkin' of sayin' anythin'?" Isbell demanded, with an aggrieved glare. "But it'll pop up; I know that! He'll say somethin' if we don't. You can't keep a thing like this out of yore conversation forever."

They had learned enough to know for a certainty that the Morgan gang had been waiting at the Turkey Creek tank for Number Four. Obviously, Belle had reached them in time with her warning.

Huck and Lafe could hold that knowledge to themselves, but it was impossible to conceal or deny the fact that Morgan and Belle had ridden into Magoffin the following night and been married. There was nothing in the Guthrie and Oklahoma City papers about it. The colonel's friends, Ben Small among them, had seen to that.

Bill Woodhall had returned to the ranch. Despite Doc Wasson's warning to him that if he did anything to enrage his father in his present condition it might prove fatal to the colonel, Bill had found a cruel satisfaction in shamelessly admitting he had been spying on Belle and kept silent in the hope she would run off with Morgan. Huck had got the facts from Doc.

"Somebody ought to be able to stop that young punk!" Lafe muttered wrathfully as Bill Woodhall rode past the hotel and went into Simmons's store. "If I was the colonel, I'd make him clear out, and for good!"

"He's all Zach's got now, Lafe. He can't do it."

"The hell he can't!" the little man contradicted. "Havin' him is a hundred times worse'n havin' nuthin'! I reckon old Zach knows he's got to git back on his feet whether he's got a bad heart or not. If he passes out, Woodhall Ranch will go to pieces in a year or two. Bill could never hold it together; what he didn't throw away, he'd lose gamblin'."

They went to bed hoping Dick would be up in the morning. The case in Guthrie concerned two men who had been caught selling whisky on the Kaw reservation. The evidence against them was such that it should not take more than a day or two to get a conviction.

Another 24 hours passed, however, before Marr reached Woodhall. He had himself in hand, but Huck and Lafe found him changed. The ever present promise of a smile no longer hovered on his mouth. There was a cold, preoccupied light in his gray eyes. He called his men together and told them they were going to pick up where they had left off.

"We've got a job to do and we'll stick at it until it's finished. I don't intend to let anything get in the way of that. I suppose you've learned that the Morgans were all set to stop Number Four the other night."

Huck acknowledged that they had.

"Well, they'll have a try at something else," Dick declared grimly. "We've been sold out two or three times, but there's no reason for us to be discouraged; Morgan will make some mistakes too."

He inquired about the colonel. They told him what they had learned from Wasson.

"He'll be okay, Doc says, if he'll take things easy," Huck stated. "But he can't stand no more of these blowups. He'll shore be glad to see you."

Marr went over to the ranch in the morning. He found old Zach sprawled out in his favorite chair on the gallery, with Ned hovering about him solicitously. Though he looked crushed, some of his old fire still burned in his eyes. He proved it a few minutes after Dick sat down with him by snapping at the faithful Ned.

"Good grief, are you going to keep fussing around me like some clucking hen for the rest of the morning?" he demanded irascibly. "Clear out of here and let Dick and me talk!"

"Yah suh, Colonel, Ah leaves yuh alone!" the old black exclaimed, giving Marr an appealing glance as he backed toward the door. "Yuh gotta res' like the doctor tol' yuh."

"I'll keep him quiet, Ned," Dick promised.

"Fiddlesticks!" Zach grumbled, when the two of them were alone. "If I listened to that old fool and Doc Wasson they'd have me under the sod before I could turn around! I'm going to go on, Dick— not like I used to, but I'm not folding up yet for a while. Thank the Lord I've got Terhune to ramrod this outfit for me while I'm getting my feet back on the ground."

"It's the slack season," Dick said. "With summer coming on, Terhune can handle things easily enough. Ross has made you a good foreman. You can depend on him."

"That's more than can be said of my own flesh and blood." Colonel Woodhall shook his head, trying to beat off the bitter thoughts that assailed him. "It's bad enough when you raise a son and see him turn out to be worthless; but it doesn't hit you all at once—you see it coming a long way off and you get set for it. It hurts, but you can keep your head up; it happens so often that, somehow, you don't feel shamed in front of the whole world. That's the way it's been with Bill. But no matter how bad things got, I could always tell myself I had Belle. I haven't anyone now.

"Don't think I'm asking for pity, Dick!" he flared up bitterly. "I'll clean the slate without any of that! Bill's got to leave! That's the first thing! There's no room for him here any more. He knew all about Belle and Morgan, and he kept his mouth shut, hoping things would turn out as they did. I told him last night if he didn't take the money I'm willing to give him and pull out for good that I'd cut him out of my will without a cent."

He had little to say about Belle. Marr could see how hard it was for him to speak of her. Though Zach couldn't forgive her for what she had done, his wrath was directed almost solely against Morgan. With his eyes flaming with implacable vengeance, he voiced his hatred of Britt. "Just killing him won't satisfy me! When I think of the life he'll lead Belle, I want to tear the very guts out of him!" He was so violent that Dick had to caution him to be careful how he excited himself.

"How can you expect me to hold myself in?" thundered Zach. It brought old Ned hurrying to the door. "You know it won't be any time before Morgan has her riding with his gang! You'll be hunting her down, along with the rest of them!"

Marr regarded it as so probable as to be almost a certainty. He was convinced it was only a question of time when he would hear that Belle had ridden in to some town with Morgan's outlaws and cracked a bank. The thrill and adventure of it would rub out any other consideration in her mind. The hot breath of danger would only add spice to it, and knowing she was putting herself outside the law wouldn't hold her back. That would be but the beginning. He would have to regard her as he would any other outlaw, with death or prison the only alternatives in the end.

"I'll cross that bridge when I come to it," he said, for though he couldn't deny the truth to himself he proposed to spare old Zach if he could. "Doolin had a wife. She was a good woman; she never got mixed up in any lawlessness. I don't know why Belle should. It doesn't follow, just because she's married to an outlaw."

"That's just talk for my benefit!" the colonel muttered without looking up. "You know better, Dick! Belle declared herself; you heard her that night. The only way to stop her is to stop Morgan. Rub him out! Smash his gang! I'll take a hand in that. I've got a big crew—twenty men! Every one of them is riding with a rifle under his leg. My orders are to shoot Morgan on sight. There's work to be done; Terhune can't spare them all, but he's got five men watching the river. If the Morgans want to run into a gun fight, let 'em try to cross my range again!"

It was exactly what Marr wanted to hear, and he did not try to conceal his satisfaction. "Your support can't help but strengthen my hand, Colonel. You can close a long stretch of the river to them."

"I'll do more than that! I don't know what your plans are, Dick. But if you find you need help, get word to me in a hurry!"

Bill Woodhall left the ranch the following afternoon, bound for some unknown destination in Texas. Huck and Lafe said it was good riddance, and Dick agreed with them, though it was his unvoiced opinion that the colonel had not seen the last of him; when he ran through his money, he'd be back for more.

Lacking a day, two weeks passed without bringing any news of the Morgans, when, toward sunset, Ri Carver drove into Woodhall in his familiar covered wagon. He stopped at Simmons's store and bought a few groceries, which he didn't need, his real purpose being to make sure the marshal knew of his presence in town. He was on his way home to Bowie. After pulling out on the Bowie road for a mile, he camped for the night. He had barely got supper started when Marr rode up to his fire. Carver, a whiskered, unsmiling man, greeted him as casually as though only a day or two had intervened since their last meeting. He had returned from his long trip beyond the Cimarron as full of information as a country newspaper, and it was all of a nature to claim the marshal's complete attention. According to Carver, the Morgan gang had its headquarters at Spanish Fort, on Rock Creek, close to the North Fork of the Canadian.

Spanish Fort was just a name for an old trading post dating back to the days of the Santa Fe trade. The original adobe "fort" had long since fallen to ruin. There were several frame buildings there now, themselves old, one a store and another masquerading as a hotel. There was a small cow outfit, known as the Spanish Ranch, near by. The two Mehaffey brothers, who ran it, made a business of buying rustled cattle and had often been accused of swinging the wide loop themselves.

"I didn't think they were that far north," Dick said. "We chased them to the North Fork after the Kansas raid, but that was well below Rock Creek."

"That's where they are," Carver repeated. "They've got the run of the Fort. Reb Santee and Cherry got mussed up at Sumner. Younger wasn't with them on that job. But they're all fit to ride again. Morgan and his wife are living at the ranch. They got back from their honeymoon about a week ago. Do you know where they went?"

"No."

"Excelsior Springs. Morgan dressed himself up like a preacher. He laughed about it to me; said nobody recognized him."

Dick asked if he had seen Belle. Carver said no.

"I didn't go to the ranch. Morgan had a list of the things she wanted."

Carver raked the glowing coals together and began to fry a piece of beef.

"I don't know what an intelligent girl like Belle Woodhall was thinking of to run off and marry him," he declared thoughtfully. "But good gravy, I've been around long enough to know there's no rhyme or reason to what a woman will do! If there was, they wouldn't be marrying the no-accounts they do. He'll walk out on her same as he's walked out on other women. He had a full-blood Cherokee girl about two years ago. He claimed he was married to her. If he was, he still is; he was never divorced that I know of. Will you have supper with me?"

"Smells good," said Dick. "I think I will sit down with you, Ri."

Carver nodded. "You'll find a can of peaches on the tailboard of the wagon. Open them up, and slice up that loaf of bread. Coffee's boiling already. Meat and potatoes will be done in a couple minutes."

When their plates and cups were filled, they sat down on the grass. Marr had shared many meals with big Ri and knew his habits. He bowed his head and waited.

"Bless this food we are about to receive from Thy bounty, O Lord!" Carver intoned humbly. Though he had not tasted food since sunrise, he ate slowly and methodically, as he did everything else.

"I saw a list of the men Morgan had with him at Manatee," he said. "Guess it was in the Wahuska paper. Every one of them has a reputation—if you want to call it that."

"How many men has he with him at the Fort, Ri?"

"I counted ten. Two or three are just hangers-on. Kiowa Jackson is the only one I saw who wasn't at Manatee that will interest you."

"Kiowa, eh?" Dick echoed. "He hasn't been out of the Canon City pen more than a month. He's always been bad luck for every bunch he's trailed with. I guess Morgan isn't superstitious."

They kept up a running conversation as they ate.

"I wish I had some really important news for you," Ri remarked, as he stacked the dishes and put some water on the fire to heat. "They've got something coming up. I don't know what it is; but it will be soon. I've never found that breed of men hard to read. Tempers get short and they begin snapping at each other when they're getting ready to ride. Some of Morgan's old hands don't like the idea of a woman mixing in. They'll leave Belle behind if Mulvey and old Buck have their way."

"I hope they do!" Marr exclaimed fervently. "Is it possible Morgan is insisting on taking Belle along?"

"I don't believe it's Morgan who's doing the insisting," Ri answered. "I think it's Belle's idea. I miss my guess if she married Morgan to be left waiting somewhere. But that's just my opinion. How many men have you got with you?"

"Five, including myself."

Carver nodded phlegmatically. "That's none too many. I don't have to tell you it would be foolish to try to round them up at the Fort; they'd know you were coming before you got halfway, and they'd fade out. Morgan has spread some money around, and an outlaw dollar looks as good as an honest one to most men out there."

It was all so true that Dick didn't even attempt to contradict it. He offered to give Ri a hand with the dishes, but the big man said no.

"You get back to town," he advised. "I won't be going out again before next month. By that time things may have changed. If they haven't, I'll get word to you if I hear anything."

Marr sat up half the night mulling over what he had learned. In the morning he contacted fully a score of local marshals and county sheriffs by telegraph, warning them to expect a raid. Most of them answered, assuring him they were on the alert.

"Sounds like you figgered somethin' might break today," Huck observed, when the marshal ordered him to stick close to the telegraph. "Keepin' our hosses standin' at the rail and sendin' me over to the depot makes it plain enough."

"Today or tomorrow or the next day is all the same, Huck," Dick answered. "We're going to be ready. You stay at the depot until I relieve you at noon. If there's a break, that's where we'll hear about it first."

Noontime came without bringing any hint of trouble. After he had had his dinner, the marshal took Huck's place in the railroad agent's office and tried to focus his attention on a magazine.

It was after three o'clock when the "sounder" began to clatter out a message. Bannister seized a pencil and wrote rapidly.

"Maybe this is what you're waitin' for!" was his excited cry. "Listen to this. That was the operator at Orlando. He says the wire has gone dead between him and Perry. The Santa Fe had a train due in Orlando ten minutes ago. It hasn't arrived, though it was on time when it left Perry."

Marr popped out of his chair, in no doubt as to what it meant.

"That wire was cut!" Bannister declared shrilly. "That train's been stopped in broad daylight, Marshal!"

"Check with the Orlando operator on when it

left Perry and when he noticed the wire had gone out!" Marr ordered.

Bannister had the information in a few minutes. The southbound Santa Fe train had pulled out of Perry at two-fifty-five. The wire had failed a minute or two after three o'clock.

"Sounds like they stuck her up about halfway between Perry and Orlando!" Dick rapped. "The Plum Creek curve, no doubt! Let me take that pencil, Jeff. Get this message off to Rossiter, at Wahuska."

Officially, Wahuska's town marshal had no authority beyond the town line, but in an emergency, jurisdictional rights wouldn't hold him back. Marr told him what had happened and ordered him to gather as many reliable men as he could in a hurry and proceed up Trapper's Creek, in the direction of the Turkey Track and Circle V ranches, and to hold that line until further notice.

"I'll be back before I pull out of town!" he called to the agent.

He ran over to the hotel and rounded up Huck and the others. His news electrified them.

"The four of you meet me at the depot in ten minutes! I'm going to see the colonel!"

Swinging up on his long-legged bay, Marr flashed away in the direction of Woodhall Ranch.

The colonel was up and about again, but it was being slowly made clear to him that the boundless vigor, which had been his for so long, had deserted him. He was on his way up from the barns, his shoulders sagging dejectedly, when Marr rode in. He brightened on catching sight of the marshal. A haggard look crept into his face as he listened to what the latter had to tell him.

"You told me I could count on your help, Colonel. I'm not asking you for a couple of men; I want you to pull your whole crew off the work and have Terhune place them so that Morgan won't have a chance to break through in this direction. The Turkey Creek bottoms will have to be blocked off. Watch the road out of Magoffin. You can spread the rest of your punchers northward along the Rock Island. With my men, I'm going to swing up that way for a couple miles and then turn east. I've got Clem Rossiter and a posse moving up Trapper's Creek. I figure that between us we can make it impossible for the Morgans to get through to the river without being shot up."

Zach regarded him with a tortured look in his eyes. "Dick—is Belle with them?"

"I don't know," Marr answered soberly. "I have some reason to believe she isn't. But whether she is or is not, Colonel, I'm going to nail them if I can; it's the only way!"

Colonel Woodhall nodded stonily and walked over to the ranch bell. He gave the rope a tug that set the bell to clanging. In a voice that was toneless, he said, "I'll hold up my end. You can count on that."

When he got back to the depot Marr found his men mounted and waiting impatiently to be off. Jeff Bannister ran across the platform, waving a telegram.

"Here's a message from Sheriff Logan, Marshal! The only way he could reach you from Perry was by way of Blackwell and Enid! Took a little time! That train was stuck up, all right!"

Dick read the wire from the Noble County sheriff aloud. Logan said he was leaving Perry with a posse of a dozen men and, striking southwest in an attempt to turn the Morgans back and bottle them up.

"That plugs the last hole!" Lafe Roberts jerked out. "It cuts 'em off on three sides! Morgan's overplayed his hand this time!"

Marr nodded, tight of lip. "Let's ride!" he called out.

Chapter Eight:
HOLED UP

THEY LEFT the Woodhall-Wahuska road several miles south of where they had stopped Lem Shoup and his wagon, and struck off to the east. It was open prairie country, almost devoid of cover, and they did not spare their horses.

According to Marr's calculations, they were far more likely to run into the bandits than Rossiter, moving up Trapper's Creek, or Eph Logan, coming down from Perry. He doubted that Morgan would try to squeeze through north of Bowie. Britt would be sure to realize that with the arrival of the looted train in Orlando the news of the robbery would be flashed to Bowie; that the town would be aroused against him long before he could pass it. He might swing to the south, but that seemed unlikely, considering the numerous towns and ranches that lay in that direction.

Marr's field marshals had been doing some figuring too, especially hardheaded little Lafe Roberts. It was his opinion that every passing minute was reducing the distance between the bandits and themselves. He expected the showdown to come a little west of the Rock Island branch line up to Manatee. He expressed himself as they toiled along. Huck was the only dissenter.

"They'll make better time than that if they're headed this way!" he declared. "We're likely to bump into 'em in the next two or three miles!"

They had barely proceeded another three miles when they saw a group of hard-riding horsemen pour over a distant rise. It seemed to confirm Huck's prediction.

Marr called a halt at once.

"Dick, there's too many of 'em to be the Morgans!" Lafe exclaimed.

"You're right, Lafe! It's Logan and his posse!"

In another moment or two Huck had to admit it was the Noble County sheriff and his men. "They shore got here in a hurry," he grumbled. "I hope it doesn't mean they've given Morgan a chance to slip around in back of 'em."

Logan rode up.

"Have you seen anything of them, Eph?" Marr asked.

"Not a thing. They've evidently decided they can't get through this way."

In appearance, there was little about Eph Logan to recommend him as a frontier sheriff, for he was a frail, emaciated man, with the dry lips of a consumptive, and as mild-mannered and colorless as an old hat. It had led some lawbreakers to hold him cheaply. They had soon learned their mistake; that under the surface Logan was all steel and bulldog grit.

"We left Perry almost as soon as we learned that

the train had been stopped," he went on. "Rufe Perry is out with a bunch from Manatee. We ran into him a long way back. I told Rufe we'd head down this way until we saw something of you. It looks to me as though we have Morgan cut off."

"I think we have," Marr agreed. "Rossiter is moving up Trapper's Creek with some men; that plugs a bad hole. We won't wait for him to join us; we'll get word to Rufe that we're moving toward Orlando and that he is to be the northern end of the dragnet. Colonel Woodhall has his entire crew out to block escape in that quarter. Pick out one of your men who can find Rufe, and get him started. If you'll turn the rest of your posse around, Eph, we'll get moving. We'll spread out some; you keep to the left of us."

When they made contact with Perry, Marr sent word along the line to spread out even more. With a little better than 50 yards separating each man from the next, it gave him a drag that measured a full 3 miles from tip to tip. Three quick shots would be a signal to close up, and it was to be repeated until every man heard it.

Marr's hopes were high as they moved forward, combing out every patch of brush and trees and making sure that no house or barn in their path concealed the bandits. When they had covered about five miles, he gave the order to wheel off to the southeast. Lafe rode at his right. They found an opportunity to exchange a word.

"I don't know, Dick!" the little man declared dubiously. "I can't believe we're pushin' them back ahead of us. We've come a long ways; we're squarely between Orlando and Bowie. If we had turned them around, we'd most likely have picked up some sign by now."

"Go on!" Dick urged. "What's your idea?"

"I think they've holed up somewheres and are waitin' for dark."

Dick regarded him thoughtfully for a moment. "You weren't of that opinion when we met Logan."

"I've changed my mind," Lafe admitted. He glanced over his shoulder at the sun and found it still high. "I never was one to stick to an opinion after I found it wouldn't hold water. I think Morgan had his retreat planned and got to the hide-out he figgered on as soon as he could. How can you see it any other way?"

"I don't know as I do," Marr replied. "All I'm sure of is that they haven't slipped past us. If they're holed up somewhere, all the better; we'll dig them out before dark."

Half an hour later he saw Lafe pull up at the face of a shallow cut-bank, and then motion for him to join him.

"Dick, look at them tracks!" the little man jerked out tensely. "They ain't more'n three or four hours old! They're as sharp as can be! Look at the edges!"

They had no difficulty in determining the direction in which the tracks led. Off to Huck Isbell's right, they could see the roof of a small ranch house.

"That's the old Pot Hook outfit in there," said Dick. "The riders who made these tracks were heading straight for it. You better hustle over to Huck and tell him to watch his step. If the Morgans are—" The sentence went unfinished as the flat crack of a rifle reached them. "That was a shot!"

"It shore was!" Lafe barked. "And there's three more from Huck! By cripes, he's found 'em!"

He repeated the signal and heard it passed along the line. He had to use his spurs to overtake Marr.

"Hit the ground and git them broncs outa here!" Huck yelled at them as they came up. He had flattened out in a little arroyo that wasn't deep enough to protect a horse. "This is the Morgans, and no foolin'!"

Lafe gathered up the animals, and with half a dozen slugs whining around his head, ran them to safety. Marr had leaped into the arroyo with Huck.

"Where did that first shot come from?" he asked.

"From the kitchen window! Whoever fired at me didn't allow for the wind or he'd have got me in the belly! It was that close, Dick! I was shore glad to find this arroyo!"

"Are they all in the house?"

"No, some are in the barn. I saw one of 'em run across the yard as I was yankin' my rifle out of the boot! I'd swear it was Younger!"

From the corner of the house someone opened fire on them, the slugs kicking up little puffs of dust within several feet of their heads.

"That's gettin' too close for comfort!" Huck growled. He shoved his rifle over the lip of the arroyo. "If that gent sticks his nose around the corner of the house again, I'll tickle it for him!"

Whoever was sniping at them soon had a fresh clip of cartridges in his rifle and started banging away again. Huck was about to snap a shot at him when a man darted out of the kitchen door and raced toward the barn. The meaning of the shooting from the corner of the house instantly became clear to Huck, and though he ran the risk of being picked off, he jerked to his feet and trained his sights on the bandit dashing across the yard. His shot lifted the man off his feet and turned him around in mid-air. He was dead when he hit the ground.

"By grab," Huck growled, "there won't be no more sass out of you!"

"Keep them penned up," Marr admonished. "They'll make a break if they reach their horses. Here comes some help."

Lafe dodged down the arroyo with Bryan and Curry.

"Huck just dropped one," Marr told them. "I'm

going to leave the four of you here for a few minutes and tell Logan and Perry what I want them to do. We'll throw a ring around the house and barn."

"You can't do it on the lower side!" Huck insisted. "It's all flat ground without a crack in it deep enough for a flea to crawl into! Any man who creeps out on that flat will have the clothes shot off him!"

"We'll seal them off some way!" Dick snapped.

He told Rufe and the sheriff how he wanted them to dispose of their men. Logan was to continue on to the right; Rufe was to get into position in the other direction.

"There's a flat on the lower side of the house and barn," he said. "It's fully half a mile wide. Don't let your boys toss their lives away trying to cross it. Just be sure you've got the flat blocked off. If you find any way to work in a little, do it."

"That arrangement will be all right till nightfall," Logan declared without any enthusiasm. "Once it gets dark, we won't be able to stop the Morgans from reaching their broncs. As soon as they do, they'll whip across that flat like a bunch of bats out of hell. We'll hear their horses running, but before we can get enough men in front of them to stop them, they'll break through."

"They'll be some who won't make it!" was Rufe's grim rejoinder.

"One of them is down already," said Marr. "Huck dropped him with his first shot. If the others come out with their hands up, well and good. If they don't, shoot to kill every time one of them shows his face. This fight won't wipe out the Morgan gang, but we'll give their wings a good clipping! You get your men in position. I'll keep in touch with you."

He rejoined Huck and the others in the arroyo. The sniping from the house had been resumed, and they were answering it. The dead man lay huddled in the yard. Lafe said no one else had tried to reach the barn.

"But there's at least a couple of 'em in there, Dick! They was there before we came up, I reckon. They been pokin' their guns through the openings between the loose boards on our side of the barn and blasting away at us."

Scattered shots from Logan's posse began to slap into the house. In a few minutes there wasn't a pane of glass intact in any of the windows. The fire was returned by the cornered gang. To the east, the Manatee men, not to be outdone, began using their guns.

"A lot of noise, and that's about all!" Huck growled.

"It's letting Morgan know we've got him surrounded," said Marr. "I haven't heard Bryan fire a shot in ten minutes. Jim!" he called. "Are you all right?"

When he failed to get an answer, he worked his way down the arroyo and found Bryan trying to sit up. The left side of his face was covered with blood.

"What happened, Jim?"

"Slug pinged off my rifle barrel and clipped me in the head," the field marshal answered. "I must have been knocked cold for a minute. Does it amount to anything, Dick?"

Marr examined the wound and found it nothing more than a crease. He offered to bind it up, but Bryan said no.

"I'll wipe the blood off my face and let it go at that." He picked up his rifle and found it undamaged. "Somebody's climbed up on the rafters and punched a hole through the barn roof. He's the gent who nicked me. Perched up there, he can make things hot for us in this ditch."

The marshal glanced at the roof and saw where several warped shingles had been knocked off. "We'll stitch a ring around that hole and stop him in a hurry!" he rapped. "A .30-.30 slug will go through the old roof like paper!"

The concentrated fire from their five rifles promptly silenced the sniper.

"Reckon we knocked him off his perch!" little Lafe declared, with a grim chuckle. "Don't see no one rushin' to take his place!"

A man opened the kitchen door and drew a dozen shots.

"He wasn't thinkin' of goin' anywheres," Huck growled. "Jest doin' a little calculatin'."

There was an interval of half an hour or more in which not a shot sounded. Marr had often read about outlaws running out of ammunition and having no choice but to throw down their guns and walk out into the open with their hands in the air. He had never experienced anything of the sort, and he doubted that it explained the present silence from the Pot Hook house. He tried not to think of Belle being there with Morgan, but the thought kept recurring to him.

In the west, the sun hung above the horizon, a fiery red ball. The long June day was drawing to a close. He knew what the next few hours would bring: darkness; the rush from the house to the barn; the desperate attempt to win across the flat; gun flashes in the night; the running fight that would follow. Months might pass before he had the Morgans at bay again.

Gazing at the battered Pot Hook house, he was tempted to give the order to close in, then and there.

"No," he decided, "it would be too costly. I can't ask these possemen to sacrifice their lives on that sort of a gamble. I'll let Morgan make the break, but the night needn't be all in his favor; as soon as it gets dark, the five of us will move up. We won't be mounted, so we'll have to make our fight before they get out of the yard, and leave it to Rufe and Logan to handle things on the flat."

The silence from the house was shattered abruptly by a violent crashing of guns.

"Somethin's stirred up a hornet's nest on the other side!" Huck called out. "Can't see nuthin', but some of Logan's men musta bin creepin' up!"

It took Marr some time to get around to the sheriff. The latter quickly confirmed Isbell's surmise.

"I warned the fools to stand pat, but four of them had to play it their own way," he explained. "You see that old wagon box out there? They thought they could reach it and push it ahead of them right up to the door." Logan shook his head soberly. "Well, they didn't make it. Young Hollister is dead, and Pete Ducker and Stringer are badly wounded. I'm going to tie them on their horses and have someone get them into Bowie; it's nearest."

Dick helped to get the two wounded men started for town. He ordered the man who was accompanying them to stop at the first ranch and transfer them to a wagon. "It'll be late when he reaches Bowie, but it's the only way he'll get them there alive," he told Logan.

He discussed his plans with the sheriff, saying that, soon after darkness fell, with his field marshals he was going to move up to the house.

"It ain't likely you'll stop them all," Logan observed. "In fact, the shoe may be on the other foot and it'll turn out to be you fellows who get stopped. You know the chance you're taking."

Marr nodded. "That goes with the job, Eph. But to get back to what you started to say—we'll hardly grab all of them. I'll have to leave it to you and Rufe to turn back or rub out the ones who get away from us."

"I'll do my best," Logan promised grimly.

"I know you will. Stick with them as long as you can. I'll go around and have a talk with Rufe, so we'll all know what we're doing."

Chapter Nine:
EIGHT MINUS THREE

HIS PLAN FAILED to arouse any great enthusiasm in the marshal from Manatee. "You know how these hot June nights are, Dick," Rufe argued. "They're as black as ink for an hour or so, early in the evenin'. We won't see the moon till after nine. We git out there on the flat, with guns poppin' every which way, you won't know who's shootin' at who."

Rufe's reasoning was better than his grammar, and Marr was compelled to agree with him.

"I know that's true," he said, "but Morgan isn't going to wait for the moon to give him away. You're nearer to the barn than the rest of us, and you've got a little cover here. Maybe you can make them hold back. Even a few minutes will help some."

"The door's on the other end. It don't give us much of a chance."

"Forget about the door," Dick told him. "If they reach their horses, they'll pry some boards off the lower side and get out that way; they won't risk using the door. As soon as it grows dark, you begin sniping at the barn. I want you to let me have a couple men who know how to use their heads; they can take our places when we start moving in."

Accompanied by the two men Rufe recommended, he made his way back to Huck and the other marshals. The purple-and-rose afterglow was dying out of the twilight already and the gray of night was deepening.

"All I want you to do," he explained to the two possemen, "is to stick here and fire an occasional shot while we're creeping up. They'll be watching for gun flashes from this direction. It may fool them into thinking we're sitting tight."

"Jest be shore you don't clip us!" Huck growled. "Keep yore slugs high! We'll be on our bellies out there, and helpless!"

There hadn't been a shot from the barn in some time. In the house, the intermittent firing from the kitchen and the front of the building continued. In the growing darkness there was a telltale red glow every time a rifle cracked.

"Shall we git goin'?" Huck inquired woodenly.

"We'll wait a few minutes more," Marr replied. "Once we get out there, don't make the mistake of firing a shot. They'll spot us in a hurry if you do. We'll try to move up to the front porch. If we make it, we'll divide and work around to the kitchen."

During the afternoon, the name of Felix Berthold, the owner of Pot Hook, had come up several times. He had lived here for years, seldom employing more than one man. His reputation was good. For that reason, Marr hesitated to accuse him of conniving with the Morgans. Lafe brought the matter up again as they waited.

"What are you goin' to say if Berthold walks out of the house after this fracas is over and swears he didn't know nothin' till the Morgans rode in and took charge? You goin' to believe him?"

"He'll have to have a good story," Dick replied. "We may find he's been murdered. I guess we can move. Spread out a little before we climb over, and keep apart. If they discover us and we have to run, head for the house and hug the walls."

Huck and the others nodded that they understood. That was all, and they crawled out of the arroyo.

On hands and knees they advanced a yard or two, then flattened down for a moment before repeating the operation. The night was as black as any they had ever known, but when they were close to the ground they could see the house looming up ahead of them a squat, blacker shape in the darkness. A gun would spurt flame from the kitchen window or the front room at short, irregular intervals and draw an answer from the arroyo, the slugs from the kitchen whining wickedly over their heads. The fire from the front room was being directed at Logan's posse.

In a moment of silence Marr thought he heard a door open at the rear of the house. He cocked an ear intently, but a gun roared and he couldn't be sure. The house was less than 50 yards away now. He whispered to Huck, and all five began quartering toward the front of the building. Without drawing a shot, they came up to within 20 yards of the porch. Within, a rifle flashed again, and in the momentary muzzle glow they saw that the front door stood open.

The circumstance was suspicious. A night breeze was stirring; the wind could have pushed the door back. The feeling whipped through Dick, however, that the gang was in the act of pulling out and had left a couple men to cover the retreat to the barn. He didn't hesitate to make a decision; he told Huck to follow him and ordered the others to take the other side and meet in back.

Huck took the lead. The two of them were so close to the wall they could touch it. The rifle barrel that was thrust through the smashed kitchen window caught a faint reflection from something. Isbell saw it, and as he crept up he raised himself to his feet and clutched it. Whoever was holding it was caught by surprise, and had it quickly wrenched out of his hands.

Marr hurried past and found the barn door standing wide open. It had been closed the last time he saw it. Even as he stood there, waiting for Huck and the others, he heard a rush of hoofs and was vaguely aware of the blurred shape of a horse detaching itself from the side of the barn and streaking across the flat. It was quickly followed by another.

"Come on!" he yelled, realizing that caution could not serve them now. "They're getting away!"

Shots from Rufe Perry's sector were spattering that side of the barn. Marr turned away from it and darted for the wide opening of the door. Huck overtook him and began to draw ahead, firing his rifle as he ran. In the black maw of the barn a streak of flame sliced the darkness. Huck dropped, cursing as he went down.

Marr heard Lafe come pounding up with Bryan and Curry. But he was also aware of other horses breaking away across the flat. He reached the door alone, and against the opening through which the bandits were fleeing he saw one bend low in his saddle for the leap to the outside. For a second or two the man was an easy target.

"Stop!" Marr yelled. "Don't make me kill you!"

"To hell with you!" was the reckless answer.

The marshal squeezed his trigger the same instant the bandit drove his spurs home. The horse bounded through the narrow opening, but the sagging rider smashed into the boards and was torn out of his saddle. He lay on the ground, moaning until consciousness fled.

Lafe and Bryan prowled forward, but they were too late. "How many got away?" Lafe demanded furiously.

"Four—maybe five," Dick answered. "What about Huck?"

"His leg, that's all!" Pat Curry told him. "Listen to that blasting out on the flat!"

"Noise, that's all!" Lafe jerked out contemptuously. "Those possemen will git in each other's way and won't stop any bandits! But, by grab, if only four, five got out of here, Dick, we did all right! Who's that on the ground?"

"I don't know. Strike a light and see if you can find a lantern."

Roberts located a lantern. "Reb Santee!" he cried, as he got a good look at the man Marr had dropped. "He's deader than a mackerel! Morgan will miss him!"

A quick search of the barn showed them another body. The man was a stranger to them.

"Must have been him that was up on the rafters," Bryan said. "He was no spring chicken, Dick. If he was the hired man, it doesn't look good for your theory that Berthold wasn't mixed up in this."

Someone stumbled out of the house, yelling, "Don't shoot! Don't shoot!"

"It's Berthold!" Lafe exclaimed.

"Grab him," said Dick. "I'm going to have a look at Huck!"

The latter made light of his wound. "I'm madder than anythin' else!" he growled. "If my rifle hadn't gone flyin' when I fell, I'd have picked off

Frank Cherry! I saw him plain enough in a gun flash to recognize him!"

"The bullet go all the way through your leg, Huck?"

"Yeh! Don't feel like it touched a bone. I'll be okay when I git the hole washed out. Did I hear Lafe say we got Santee?"

"We did," Marr confirmed. "We'll get you into Bowie as soon as we can." He hurried over to where Lafe was questioning the owner of Pot Hook.

"He claims the Morgans tied him up," the little man told him. "I see his legs is bound. His head looks like it'd had a gun barrel laid on it. Mebbe his story *is* all right."

"What is your story, Berthold?" Dick demanded.

"I was in the kitchen, havin' somethin' to eat with Dutch Oetgen, my hired man, when they rode into the yard. I knew they was bandits soon as I saw 'em. I figgered they was the Morgans. They told me they was puttin' their broncs in the barn and takin' charge of things till midnight. I told 'em I wasn't goin' to git mixed up with them, and one of 'em clips me over the head. When I came to, I was tied up, The only one I recognized fer shore was old Buck Younger. Jest before the shootin' began, he took Dutch out to the barn to feed their broncs."

Lafe turned to Marr, his expression rather incredulous. "Dick, do you believe Buck made this Dutch climb up on them rafters and start throwin' lead at us?"

"It sounds like Buck," Marr declared. "You go on, Berthold. What happened in the last few minutes?"

"When they got ready to make their break, they untied my hands and made me sit down on the floor and start shootin' through the front window. They left one of their bunch with me to see I didn't pull no tricks. He's in the kitchen now. He's either dead or dyin'. They jest called him Kid. I didn't hear no other name for him."

"The Tulsa Kid!" Lafe muttered. "Where's the gent that Huck dropped?"

"Over here," Bryan told him.

They walked over to the huddled shape, and Lafe raised his lantern. "Kiowa Jackson!" several of them exclaimed together.

"Yeh," Marr said. "His luck didn't improve any."

They went into the kitchen then. The Tulsa Kid sat on the floor beneath the window. His eyes were glassy.

"He's done for," Bryan said, bending over him. "I guess they knew he was when they left him."

"That's what they told him," said Berthold. "Morgan told him to sit there at the winder and take a couple of you marshals with him when he kicked off. Look at this place! It's wrecked! Who's goin' to make good to me?"

"You can file a claim for damages," Marr told him. "I'll see that you get something." He asked Bryan and Lafe to bring Huck in. "I want you to hitch a team, Berthold, and take him to Bowie. How many men did Morgan have with him?"

"There was eight of 'em, all told."

"All men?" Dick asked, voice tight in his throat.

Berthold was puzzled by the question, but only for a moment. "You mean did Morgan have his wife with him?"

"Yeh."

"No, he didn't have no woman along."

He asked about his hired man. Marr told him what had happened. Berthold rubbed a horny hand across his mouth as he sat down heavily. "I knew it!" he muttered. "Don't mean much to you, I reckon, but Dutch was the best man ever worked for me. Not that I'm blamin' you for what you did; you couldn't have done any different. Guess I better put the team to the wagon."

They had Huck ready to start for Bowie in a few minutes. Dick asked Bryan to go in with him.

"The rest of us will stick here till we hear from Rufe and Logan," he said. "But we'll be in later tonight, Huck."

The wagon had been gone several hours before they heard the posse returning. They hadn't taken any prisoners. One of the Manatee men claimed he had seen an outlaw drop from his horse, only to have the gang swing back and pick him up. Rufe was disgruntled over the out-come.

"They scattered like quail as soon as they broke through us!" he complained. "Seemed to me they was headin' for Kingfisher. They could cross the river down there. If they do, Woodhall won't see anythin' of 'em."

"We don't have to apologize for what we accomplished today," Marr said quietly. "Morgan won't find any men to take the places of the ones he's lost. He'll have to fill his ranks with second- and third-raters. I don't mean that his gang is broken up. They'll keep on raiding, but they'll never ride so wide, high, and handsome again!"

Chapter Ten:
FEMININE TRIGGER FINGER

IT WAS AFTER MIDNIGHT when Marr rode into Bowie. He passed Ri Carver's house and was reminded of his indebtedness to Ri.

Bowie had quieted down with Huck Isbell's arrival and the news of what had occurred at the Pot Hook. His wound had been treated, and when Marr and Lafe reached his room in the hotel, they found him propped up in bed playing euchre with Jim Bryan.

"Where's Pat?" he asked, an edge of anxiety riding his tone.

"Don't worry; he's all right," Dick told him. "I've started him north to find Rossiter and that Wahuska bunch and let them know there's no need to stick it out any longer. He's going to meet us in Woodhall sometime tomorrow. How are you making it?"

"All right!" Huck protested. "You ain't anchorin' me here! If you don't mind, we'd like to know how things wound up." Marr and Lafe gave them the details.

"You won't be doing any riding for a week or so, Huck," said the marshal. "You catch the morning train down to Guthrie and take things easy for a while. I won't listen to any argument about it. You can believe it or not, but ten hours have passed since that Santa Fe train was stopped, and I still don't know anything about it. Some news must have reached Bowie a long while back. How much did the Morgans get?"

"About three thousand," Bryan informed him. "They stuck her up on the Plum Creek curve, just as you figured."

"And right cute they was!" Huck interjected. "A construction gang had been workin' there for a couple days and the trains had been ordered to take the curve at slow speed. When the engineer saw a man runnin' toward him, wavin' a red flag, he slapped on the brakes. He looked ahead and saw a pile of ties on the track. The next thing he knew, the Morgan gang was racin' down that slope above the curve and slappin' lead into the train. It was all over in about ten minutes."

"Anyone get hurt?" Dick inquired.

"No! The train crew didn't put up any argument!" Huck snorted contemptuously. "A daylight robbery! And let 'em git away with it like that! I reckon that express messenger had the door open before they could even say 'Please!'"

"Well, you say good night and get to sleep." Dick beckoned to Bryan. "You come along with us, Jim. We're going to try to find something to eat and then turn in ourselves. We'll go on to Woodhall in the morning. As for you, Huck, I don't want to see you until that leg is okay. Understand?"

"That's a lot of damnfool nonsense," Isbell grumbled. "But all right!"

Back in Woodhall, Marr learned that the Morgans had crossed the Cimarron and swung west in the direction of Watonga and the North Fork almost within sight of Kingfisher. As a result, the colonel's crew had seen nothing of them, though he had kept them out all night.

Uncle Ben came up during the day. He had a bundle of newspapers under his arm and was in a happy frame of mind. "Seems we're riding high again," he said, slapping the papers on the table in Dick's room. "I brought these along. I thought maybe you'd like to read your own press notices. I came up by way of Guthrie. Spent a couple hours there; saw Huck. It doesn't leave much for you to tell me."

Marr grinned. "It doesn't—not if you've been talking to Huck. We could have had better luck last evening."

"You gave a good account of yourselves," the old marshal declared with his usual positiveness. "Morgan knew what he was doing when he picked the Pot Hook. I've seen that house a hundred times and know it would be impossible to block it off on the south side. I was sorry to hear about Gene Hollister."

"Yeh," Dick murmured regretfully. "He was just a boy, really."

Uncle Ben nodded. "They're going to bury him

139

tomorrow. I'll go up for the services; I've known his folks for years. Have you heard anything from Carver?"

Marr told him of his meeting with Ri.

"So they've been headquartering at Spanish Fort, eh?" Uncle Ben rubbed his chin reflectively. "It doesn't help much to know where the game is to be found if you can't reach it. You handed Morgan a drubbing. I hate to see him given time to lick his wounds and get set for another raid."

Dick's eyes narrowed speculatively. "Uncle Ben, are you suggesting that I make a drive on Rock Creek?"

"No, not at all! It would only be playing tag with them. Just keep your ears open, Dick, and try to clip 'em again right soon. If you do, you'll have them reeling. There's something in the ego of men like Britt Morgan that seems to take charge of them when they've been handed a licking. They've just got to show the world nobody's got them down. You're the man he'll be out to prove that to, and he won't wait too long, Dick! He'll pick out something that looks easy and try to do it up in spectacular fashion."

Marr found Uncle Ben's estimate of Morgan coinciding perfectly with his own. "I believe that as strongly as you do," he said. "It wouldn't satisfy him to hoist a bank in some faraway corner of the country; he'll try to rub my nose in it.

Chances are it will be some town north and east of Wahuska; we've made things a little too hot for him down here."

Small nodded. "You've also proved to me that making your headquarters here was a shrewd move."

Lafe came in with Bryan and Curry, and they sat down and joined in the conversation. Uncle Ben shook his head over what Dick had to say about the colonel.

"I don't suppose the ranch is the same," he said, his tone sober and sad.

"No, and it never will be again," Dick returned. "It's like Ned said: there's nothing left of Woodhall Ranch as it used to be but a broken old man and some memories." His mouth tightened unconsciously. "It got to me pretty hard, the way he put it. I've thought of it a dozen times."

"It tears your heart out to see a fine, upstanding man like Zach Woodhall struck down this way." The old marshal spoke with deep feeling. "There's nothing could have happened to him that would have hurt half so much as this foolishness of Belle's. I knew he was crushed when he wrote Skidmore that he wouldn't be down for the parade. Gil showed me the letter. Zach just said he couldn't face all those people. I filled in for him; it was the first time in twelve years he wasn't grand marshal. There must have been a hundred people tell me the parade didn't seem the same without him. I didn't feel right all along the line of march; it was like I was taking a dead man's place."

Uncle Ben got to his feet and froze the emotion out of his round face. "Have you seen him today, Dick?"

"No, I haven't."

"Put on your hat, then. We'll go over and cheer him up a little if we can."

Small found the change in the colonel so great that it was an effort for him to pretend to be unaware of it and muster the laughter and bantering tone he knew Zach had come to expect from him.

The colonel seemed to be acquainted with the outcome of the fight at the Pot Hook. "I don't feel very chipper today," he admitted. "I was up all night, hoping we'd be of some help."

"You helped a lot," Dick assured him. "You made it possible for me to forget about Woodhall and head east. I didn't mean for you personally to take a hand. I figured Ross Terhune would handle things."

Zach said, "I had to get in it. I couldn't stand being cooped up. Maybe we'll do better the next time."

Black Ned was as pleased to see Marr and Uncle Ben as the colonel. He mixed some drinks and urged them to stay for supper. "Lak ole times, seein' de two of yuh here together," he chattered.

"Ah kin promise yuh gen'men ranch-cured ham and fresh greens from de gahden."

"Course we'll stay," the old marshal answered for himself and Marr. "I don't get up to Woodhall Ranch every day."

Pathetically, the colonel asked about the parade, and Uncle Ben told him how he had been missed.

"You'll have to make it next year, Zach. I was in the saddle from eight o'clock on to noon. The parade didn't get moving until ten o'clock. That was more riding than I've done in three years. I was stiff for a couple days. I want you to promise me right now that we can depend on you next year."

"Well, we'll see," Zach murmured, pleased to learn that he had been missed.

Despite Marshal Small's best efforts, supper dragged. Later, seated on the gallery as he waited for the night train south, he caught the colonel nodding several times. He looked feeble and worn.

"Never mentioned Belle once," Uncle Ben got out soberly, as he walked back to the depot with Marr. "He isn't going to last long, Dick. In some ways it would be a blessing if he went quickly."

Marr looked up. "Just how do you mean that, Uncle Ben?"

"I suppose the ranch will be left to Belle and her brother. She isn't outside the law yet; she could claim her interest and prevent Bill from running through it. That won't be the case if she gets involved in a felony and has to keep on the dodge with Morgan. Someone will have to take charge of the ranch, and the court will recognize Bill. If you could see Belle and tell her how things are with her father and that she stands to lose everything if her brother gets his fingers on the place, it might do some good."

"If I could see her?" Marr repeated. "That's a big if, Uncle Ben!"

"I suppose it is," the old marshal acknowledged gloomily. "Well, you keep me posted."

In the days that followed, Marr found little to do but wait. Huck came up from Guthrie, his leg as good as ever. He had been back a week or more, when Ri Carver drove into Woodhall. He nodded to Dick as he passed the hotel and pulled up in front of Simmons's store. Dick followed him. They greeted each other impersonally. There were several women in the store, as well as Abe Simmons, which was as Carver wanted. He could speak to the marshal in their hearing without giving anyone reason to believe they had a secret understanding.

"I'm off again," he said. "Only as far as the North Fork this trip."

"Safer for you out there than it would be for me," Dick said laughingly. "How long will you be gone?"

"Couple weeks. If business is any good, I'll

go up as far as Spanish Fort. Give me a couple pounds of sugar, when you get around to it, Abe."

Marr strolled out. Ri had told him what he wanted him to know.

Carver had been gone only three days and, at his usual rate of progress, could not have been much more than halfway to Rock Creek, when the news was flashed to Woodhall that the Morgans had ridden into Wetonka, a Rock Island town between Wahuska and Waukomis, and stuck up the bank. The place was so small that its only officer was a part-time night watchman. The wire was from him. It said they had one of the bandits cornered at a farm on the outskirts of town.

Luckily, there was a train north in twenty minutes. Marr and his field marshals armed themselves and hurried to the depot. It was only a fourteen-minute ride to Wetonka. When they started to get off the train, the Wetonka agent ran up to them. "You better stay on and I'll have the conductor let you off just north of town!" he said breathlessly. "Sickles is out there with half of Wetonka! You'll see them from the tracks!"

Matt Sickles detached himself from a group of armed men surrounding two haystacks at a healthy distance and ran up to meet the marshals.

"I was hopin' you'd catch this train!" he panted. "We got Buck Younger cornered in between them stacks! He crawled in there with a broken leg!

Train hit him when they was makin' their get-away!"

"What train hit him?" Marr snapped.

"A southbound freight! They crossed in front of it to git away from us. Younger didn't make it." Sickles was beginning to catch his breath. "His hoss was killed and he was pitched into the ditch. He's hurt; I could tell by the way he was draggin' himself along. He's lost his rifle, but he's got a Colt and plenty of ca'tridges. The Morgans wouldn't have got into the bank if we hadn't lost our wits, but the sight of that gal out there on her hoss, snappin' shots at us, and jest as cool as a cucumber, left us jest plum' flabbergasted!"

Marr stiffened and choked back a groan. "Was she masked?"

"Naw! She was purty as a picture, settin' there, her red hair flyin'. It was that Woodhall gal, shore 'nough!"

Though Dick had been trying to set himself for what he felt was bound to happen, now that he was face to face with it he was staggered.

Little Lafe Roberts understood. "Come on!" he growled. "We'll snag Younger this time, and we'll see that he stays put!"

Marr silently thanked him for the moment it gave him to pull himself together.

"Look out for him!" Sickles warned. "He'll drop you if you git close!"

Marr took off his guns and handed them to

Huck. "I'll talk to him," he said. He advanced close enough to the stacks so that he didn't have to raise his voice to make himself heard. "Buck, you're hurt; you can't get away. Throw down your gun and crawl out of there. You know you'll get a square shake from me."

"If you want me, come and git me!" the old outlaw answered defiantly.

"Okay, if that's the way you want it," Marr returned promptly. "Lafe, Huck—get around on the side and put a match to the stacks. We'll have to smoke him out."

It brought Buck to terms.

"Reckon you ain't bluffin'!" he snarled. "I'll give up!"

He came out slowly on his hands and knees. Dick told his men to keep the crowd back.

"Your leg, eh?" he said to Younger.

"Yeh, busted, an' I'm hurt inside. I need a doctor."

"You won't get one this time until I've got you in the Guthrie jail." Dick told his marshals to get Younger to the depot. "Chain him to the safe when you get him there. It'll be about an hour before the afternoon train pulls in."

With Sickles, he walked into Wetonka and questioned the banker and his clerk. The Morgans had made off with very little. "How many were in the gang?" Marr asked.

"Counting the girl, six," Sickles told him.

Dick didn't know whether to be surprised or not.

He recalled Uncle Ben's prediction that Morgan might make a raid before he had had time to rebuild his gang. On the other hand, there seemed to be some reason to believe that Britt intended to go along as he was. The matter came up on the journey to Guthrie. The marshal tried to draw an answer from old Buck.

"Where you goin' to find good men to ride with you these days?" Buck demanded morosely. "I'd rather go it alone than have some of these tinhorn saloon gladiators sidin' me! They'll fold up on you when you need 'em most! Mulvey and the others feel the same as I do about that."

He sounded gloomy and depressed. It was the first time Marr had seen him in that mood. By seven o'clock he was safely lodged in the federal jail. In addition to his injured leg, he had three broken ribs.

"We're whittlin' 'em down," Huck observed as he sat in the office with Dick after the doctor left. Lafe and the others had stepped out for supper. "You can count the Morgans on the fingers of one hand now. This Wetonka job jest about broke their backs."

"I'm afraid that's not all it broke," Dick answered, rummaging in a desk drawer for a razor and shaving mug. "The colonel knows by now that Belle took part in the raid. I dread to think of what we may hear when we get back to Woodhall in the morning."

Chapter Eleven:
A MISSION OF MERCY

JEFF BANNISTER BECKONED to Marr as the latter stepped off the morning train at Woodhall. "Doc Wasson asked me to be on the lookout for you, Marshal," he said. "He wants you to come to the ranch at once."

"The colonel?" Dick knew the question was hardly necessary. Bannister nodded gravely.

"He's pretty low, Doc says."

Lafe put his hand on Marr's arm. "Go ahead," he urged. "If anythin' turns up that you ought to know about, I'll come for you."

Black Ned was out on the gallery watering the potted plants that once had been Belle's special pride, when Dick neared the house. There was a scared, hopeless look on the aged Negro's face.

"Mawnin', Mist' Dick," he moaned. "Look lak we goin' ter lose de colonel fer shore dis time."

"Don't talk like that," Marr said gruffly, without meaning to be short with the old man. "We've got to keep our chins up."

Wasson came out of Zach's bedroom and closed the door softly. "I'm glad you're here," he said. "Sit down with me for a minute; I want to talk to you."

"It's serious, eh?" Dick got out with an effort.

Wasson snapped his fingers. "He can go like that! The news from Wetonka floored him. He's had two bad attacks. I'm feeding him a little morphine to keep him quiet. He keeps asking for Belle. He knows this is the end, and he wants to see her before he goes. Dick, would it be possible to get word to her?"

Marr shook his head slowly. "I don't see how. The only way would be for me to find her, and that wouldn't work out. There's a charge against Belle; she knows she's wanted. The Morgan gang wouldn't let me get within a country mile of her."

"What about Ri Carver?" Wasson persisted. "He doesn't seem to have any difficulty moving around out there. He could locate her for us. I saw him drive through Woodhall three or four days ago. Where was he going?"

"Out to the North Fork and as far up as Rock Creek and Spanish Fort. I imagine he'll be camping on the creek tonight. No doubt Ri could get to her."

"Then you've got to find him, Dick!" Wasson had never sounded so emphatic. "This is the last favor you'll be able to do the colonel!"

For a long moment Marr sat there lacing and unlacing his fingers and saying nothing.

"I know it's dangerous," Wasson admitted.

"I'm not thinking of that, Doc. Finding Belle is only half of it. You're asking me to give her a safe-conduct into the ranch."

"Well, is that too much to ask?" Wasson's voice rose indignantly. "There isn't an honest man in Oklahoma who won't pat you on the back for it! If you put it up to Ben Small—"

"He'd have to say no; he couldn't do otherwise!" Marr said flatly. "If I do this it will have to be on my own responsibility."

He hauled himself to his feet and walked the length of the room and back, his face rocky.

"Outlaws have always got a square deal from me," he got out gruffly. "But I don't believe in coddling them, and that's what this amounts to. I know it's a mistake even to consider it."

"But that girl isn't really an outlaw, Dick," the doctor protested. "You know—"

"She became an outlaw in my book the moment she rode into Wetonka with the rest of them and used her rifle to hold the town at bay! If she were taken into custody, she'd be sent away for at least five years for her part in that robbery!" His gray eyes glittered coldly as he faced Wasson. "Can I see the colonel?"

"He's conscious. You can see him for a minute. Whatever you do, hold out some hope to him."

Colonel Woodhall recognized Dick at once. They gazed at each other with a deep understanding, and the respect and affection that had been a bond between them for years found full expression without a word being spoken. "Don't

151

try to cheer me up," Zach said weakly. "I know this is the end of the trail, Dick. It doesn't do any good to think of what might have been; the pitcher is broken, and the pieces can't be put together. I want to see Belle—that's all. I won't scold her. I—I just feel that if I can talk to her it may bring her to her senses."

"I'll fetch her, Colonel," Marr promised, his voice husky. "I'll do all I can."

Zach thanked him with his eyes.

"Dick—if you don't get back in time—look out for Belle a little, will you?" he pleaded as the marshal started to leave the room. "Belle isn't bad, Dick—just wild."

Marr turned to Wasson when the latter had closed the bedroom door. "How long can you keep him alive?" he asked.

"Forty-eight hours maybe—if he'll help me a little," Doc answered. "I can't promise anything, of course."

"You do your best!" Dick muttered. "I'll have her here!"

He made his plans as he hurried to town. He'd take a light wagon and ask Huck to go with him. He'd leave little Lafe in charge at Woodhall. He knew he could depend on the man's judgment. It was nine o'clock now. By midnight Huck and he could be on Rock Creek. It was clouding up in the west. There was a feeling of coming rain in the air. It wouldn't slow them appreciably. Blankets and a little grub, and a tarp to cover the wagon, would be all they'd need.

He found Huck and Lafe at the livery barn, where they kept their horses. "Yo're mad to try it, Dick!" Isbell protested, when he learned what Marr proposed doing. "It might cost you yore commission!"

"No matter what it costs, I'm going," was the determined answer. "We won't accomplish anything by talking about it. You get a team hitched and borrow a tarp. Pick me up at the hotel. I'll be ready with the blankets and some food. You walk back with me, Lafe, and I'll tell you what you're to do while we're gone."

With Huck handling the reins, Dick and he pulled out of town in less than half an hour. A mongrel dog that belonged at the hotel trotted off with them. Huck tried to turn it back several times.

"Let him come along if he wants to," said Marr. "It looks innocent, having a dog with us. We may be glad we've got him."

They cut through Woodhall range to the river. The Cimarron was low and could be crossed almost anywhere. A thin, fine rain began falling as they drove through the brakes on the far side of the stream. They pulled up for a minute, and while Huck was getting his bearings Dick spread the tarp over the blankets, rifles, and grub.

"We'll quarter off to the north," said Huck. "It'll be miles shorter than lightin' out for the North Fork and followin' her to Rock Crick."

The rain continued, and the day was not only dismal but unseasonably cool for late June. They pulled into some trees at noon and ate a cold snack. Huck gave the horses a little grain.

In the course of the morning, they had passed several dugouts without stopping. When they went on, after eating, it was a long time before they caught sight of a human habitation.

"Better stop and find out if we're headin' right," Isbell advised. "I got a general idea of where I am, but there ain't no sense in a man wanderin' around on these prairies in all this wet if he don't have to."

The dog's barking gave advance notice of their coming. When they drew up at the door of the combination sod shanty and dugout, a stringy, loose-jointed man, so thin he seemed to be just skin and bones, stepped out. He ran his eye over them suspiciously.

"Do yuh know Ri Carver?" Huck asked, giving his words a hillbilly twang.

"Yup, I do," the man acknowledged.

"How long ago did he pass yore place?"

The nester appeared to think. After scratching his head, he said, " 'Bout four day ago. Yup, four day ago eggzactly!"

"We got to find him in a hurry," Huck continued,

doing all the talking for himself and Dick. "Yuh got any idear whar we kin locate him?"

The man shook his head. "Don't allow as I have, stranger."

It told Marr and Isbell that the man was lying, for Ri never made any secret of his general destination, and for the very excellent reason that if anyone needed medicine they would know where to look for him.

"That's too bad," Huck declared. "Hate to waste time lookin' fer him along the North Fork. Got a little bad news for Carver."

This piece of invention made the man waver in his determination not to give them any information. "Sunthin' wrong ter home, eh?" he inquired.

Huck nodded, sensing the other's fading suspicion. "We're obliged to yuh anyhow. We'll be movin' on. Yuh got any neighbors who might straighten us out?"

"Thar's some Jepsons to the north 'bout five mile. That'd take yuh out of yore way, I reckin. Mebbe it'd be best fer yuh ter head fer Rock Crick."

Huck shook his head and put on a blank face. "Don't know as I could find it."

"Jest keep favorin' yore left hand as yuh move along. It's a far piece. Thar's kin of mine livin' up that-a-way. When yuh see some hills ahead of yuh, swing west and yuh'll pass thar place. If

155

thar's anyone ter home, tell 'em I said ter point out the way to the crick."

Huck thanked him and drove on.

"Took him a long time to make up his mind that we weren't a couple marshals," said Dick. "That was a smart idea, asking for Ri. I never heard you going better."

Isbell bent his head and let the rain run off his hat brim. "Wal, I saw it wouldn't do to ask that snake-eyed gent the way to Rock Crick," said he.

The afternoon was half gone before they saw the hills the squatter had mentioned. They circled them to the west. An hour later they located a dugout. Huck did the talking again and succeeded in having the way to Rock Creek pointed out to him. But the directions were vague, for in this wild, almost uninhabited country there were no roads and few landmarks to guide a man; just the untamed prairie, stretching away in every direction.

"I've never seen it no colder in November!" Huck complained, as he whipped up the team. "Wish I'd had the sense to bring a bottle along. I could stand a nip, I'm tellin' you!"

They were soaked to the skin and thoroughly uncomfortable. Even the dog had lost interest in the trip and moved along at the side of the wagon with its tail between its legs.

"Stop a minute, and I'll lift the dog into the wagon," said Dick. "He can curl up under the seat.

If we've got another thirty miles to go, we'll be lucky to hit the creek by midnight."

"We'll be dang lucky it we don't git lost! It's goin' to git dark and we won't have so much as a star to go by. There won't be nothin' to do but follow our noses."

Their unfamiliarity with the country was due entirely to the fact that they were taking a short cut. Both had been along the North Fork of the Canadian many times, and far beyond Spanish Fort.

They saw no one as the afternoon waned. It was their hope to find another dugout before night fell and check on the course they were taking. They seemed doomed to be disappointed until, with evening coming on, Huck reined up sharply and pointed through a screen of blackjack scrub at a hillside on their left.

"By grief, there's a soddy!" he exclaimed. "You see it?"

Marr nodded. The two of them studied it for some minutes. "There doesn't seem to be any sign of life there," Dick remarked pessimistically.

"Someone to home!" Huck growled. "I jest caught a trace of smoke driftin' away. A fire shore would feel good!"

"You better drive up," Marr told him. "We won't be welcome, but if we're not recognized, we may get a chance to dry out a little. I'll leave it to you to do the talking."

"That dang hound will start yappin' and let 'em know we're coming as soon as we git out in the open, same as he's done all day," Isbell complained. He clucked his tongue at the team. "If anybody is inclined to knock us off this wagon, it gives him plenty time to make up his mind!"

"Don't worry about the dog," Dick retorted. "His barking may have saved our skins a couple times today. Traveling by wagon and having the pup along still strikes me as a good idea. I know we'd never have got this far on horseback without being sniped at."

The dog began to bark, as Huck predicted, and kept it up until the wagon reached the door. No one stepped out to hail them. It sharpened suspicion in the lanky Isbell in an instant.

"I'll get down and try the door," Marr told him.

"You better have yore rifle on yore arm!" Huck cautioned.

The marshal said no. He rapped sharply on the door. Getting no answer, he pushed it open. A murmur of voices died abruptly as he stepped in. Double bunks, curtained with gunny sacking, enough to sleep a dozen men, lined both sides of the room. At the far end, seated in front of an open fire that illumined the room, he saw a ragged, hairy-looking individual. A rifle stood against the fireplace at his elbow. He said nothing, but his narrowed, hostile eyes followed Dick as the latter advanced toward him.

Marr knew what he had stepped into. The Morgans were no longer on Rock Creek. They were here in this dugout—all of them, perhaps even Belle. He shuddered at the thought that she had brought herself to this.

His nerve had often been tested, and it did not fail him now. He knew it was too late to turn back; that behind those flimsy curtains guns were leveled at him. Though he didn't know how he was to get out alive, he walked up to the fire and turned his back to it to warm himself, acting as casually as though he were back at Woodhall Ranch.

"Cold rain," he said to the man on the stool.

The latter did not move a muscle. He said, with dire meaning, "Yuh git out of here the same way you git in—by that door!"

Marr understood him and was certain he would be shot down long before he reached the door.

"You know me, so I better speak my piece," he said. "If you're in sound of my voice, Britt, listen to me. The colonel is dying. The doctor gives him no more than forty-eight hours. They called me to the ranch this morning. The colonel wants to see Belle. I promised him I'd try to find her. If you'll bring her to the river, I'll be waiting on the other side at the ranch crossing and take her in and bring her back to you. All I ask is that you make no attempt to cross the river yourself. If you'll give me your word, I'll promise you you'll be safe."

"You're a fool if you listen to him!" someone snarled. It sounded like the scratchy, rasping voice of Arkansaw Bob. "He'll trap you, Morgan! All you've got is his word for it that old Woodhall is dyin'!"

"That's the dumbest damn thing I ever did hear!" another boomed. Dick knew it was Link Mulvey. "If Marr gives you his word, you can count on it, Britt!"

One of the curtains was tossed aside, and Morgan rolled out of his bunk. He was unshaven, disheveled, and anything but the debonair figure he had been that night at Woodhall Ranch. His left arm was bandaged. It could have been an old wound, suffered in the battle at the Pot Hook. Most likely, it went back no further than yesterday, at Wetonka.

"Let's hear a little more of your piece," Morgan invited, his tone cold and menacing. "How did you know you'd find us here?"

Marr shrugged enigmatically. "You have your ways of getting information and so have I, Morgan." He was in no danger of acknowledging that he had blundered into the hide-out by mistake; that if the man at the fireplace had only come to the door, Huck and he would have driven on, none the wiser. "Is Belle hearing what I'm saying?"

"She's not here." Britt regarded him with a bitter enmity. "You took Younger in?"

"I've got him in Guthrie. He's got a broken leg and three fractured ribs—if nothing more. Buck's earned a long rest."

There was an uneasy stirring behind the curtains as Mulvey, Cherry, and Arkansaw Bob took stock of the future. Rep Santee, Kiowa Jackson, the Tulsa Kid all killed! Old Buck a prisoner! An echo of what the men in the bunks were thinking was reflected for a fleeting second on Morgan's face.

"I couldn't get Belle there tonight," he declared sullenly. "If late tomorrow afternoon will do—"

"It will have to do," Marr said. "I'll be waiting."

Morgan stepped aside to let him pass. He had almost reached the door when there was a scuffle behind him.

"Throw down that gun, yuh dirty ole sneak!" Link Mulvey barked.

"But yo're lettin' him git away!" the owner of the dugout whined. "I left him fer you fellas to git and now yo're—"

"Shut up and drop that gun!" Link's voice trembled with fury. "I ain't seein' a man shot in the back when he's tryin' to do one of us a favor!"

Dick climbed into the wagon and told Huck to drive on. "Don't look back," he said tensely. "They're all in there—Morgan and his whole bunch."

"Belle, too?"

Marr shook his head. "Thank the Lord, she isn't! Britt's promised to bring her to Woodhall Crossing tomorrow afternoon. You can swing the team in the other direction; we'll keep moving until we reach the river."

"And without losin' any time!" was Isbell's sober rejoinder. "Somebody back there might change his mind about pottin' us!"

His teeth chattered as a chill racked him. The dog rubbed against his leg and looked up at him quizzically.

"Yeh, I know yo're a good dog!" Huck muttered. "Reckon if it hadn't been for yore yappin' we'd have a different story to tell!"

"We'd have been cut down," Marr said grimly.

Chapter Twelve:
DEATH INTERCEDES

MARR FOUND the colonel about the same as when he left, though Wasson said Zach was weaker.

"But he'll hang on, now that he knows she's coming. How long are you going to give Belle with her father?"

"As long as she wants. If anyone comes to the house while I'm down at the river waiting for her, make some excuse that will send them away."

"You can depend on that," Doc told him.

Dick had to take Ross Terhune, the foreman, into his confidence. Terhune was surprised, as well as moved, to learn that Belle was coming in.

"I don't know how much this will mean to Miss Belle—a great deal, I imagine—but I know it's the greatest favor anyone ever did the colonel. I've been going around in a daze. I know when he goes it will be the end of everything here for me. I could never work for Bill."

"Maybe you won't have to, Ross. There's a chance—just a slim one—that Belle may see things differently when she's had a talk with her father. Now I want you to keep the crew away from the river this afternoon and evening. I don't want the men hanging around the yard, either."

"I'll see to it," Terhune said. "I can arrange

some work that will keep them out of the way."

It was still early when Dick rode down to the river. The ranch crossing was little more than a mile from the house. Through the years, the approach to it had been carved deep by the hoofs of horses and cattle. When Woodhall livestock strayed, it was usually across the Cimarron. It was from the crossing that the colonel's punchers always set out to round up the strays. As a result, trails and openings had been worn through the junglelike brakes.

The amount of time Morgan had said he'd need to bring Belle to the river left little doubt in Dick's mind that she was at the Spanish Fort ranch. He took it for granted that the gang had quitted the dugout soon after Huck and he had driven away. The place had no future interest for him, for he knew it would stand deserted until some nester family appropriated it for their own.

Though he saw Morgan as reaching Spanish Fort by midnight, he doubted that Britt had turned back with Belle before morning. Marr shook his head dubiously as he tried to calculate the distance they had to come.

"It's a long, hard day's riding!" he told himself. "They won't come too fast; Britt will be thinking of the horses and trying to keep them fresh enough for a getaway if something should go wrong. If I see anything of them before evening, I'll be surprised!"

The afternoon seemed to drag on interminably. The rain had passed, but the sky was still overcast. He found his thoughts as drab and bleak as the day.

"Four o'clock!" he murmured, glancing at his watch. "It'll be another hour, at least."

He refused to let his thoughts dwell on the possible consequences to himself of permitting Belle to see her father. He was satisfied it could not be kept a secret and that it would be foolish to attempt any denial of his part in it. He had been confident all afternoon that Morgan would bring her to the crossing. Doubt began to gnaw at him, however, when five o'clock passed without any sign of them.

Wasson had promised to send word to him if there was any change in the colonel's condition. He glanced toward the house every few minutes, but he saw no one coming.

Thanks to the gray day, it began to grow dark in the willow brakes in the river bottom earlier than usual. Repeatedly he left his horse and walked to the water's edge, listening carefully for the sound of snapping limbs and dead brush that would tell him they were coming. He failed to catch any sound. The Cimarron flowed along in somber silence.

Marr had been staring at it abstractedly for several minutes when a movement across the river caught his eye. He looked up to see Belle riding up to the ford. She crossed without hesitation. If Morgan was with her, he did not show himself.

"Am I in time, Dick?" she asked anxiously.

"Yes," he told her. "I'll take you to the house right away."

He noticed she was still using her favorite sidesaddle, though her mount did not wear the Flying W that was the Woodhall brand. Her riding skirt and gray whipcord jacket looked familiar. Indeed, Dick found her changed very little. If she looked tired, he knew it was only because she had just finished a ride that would have taxed the strength of most men. Her skin had all its peach-bloom loveliness and her red hair a sheen that the dull day could not erase.

"You're not armed, Belle?" he asked.

"No." It was just a tense whisper.

Marr had thought of so many things he wanted to say to her, but now that she was here he could find nothing that he felt free to voice.

For her part Belle was equally reticent. They were halfway to the house before she said, "No one else would have done this for me, Dick. I want you to know I appreciate it. But you've always been that way. If anyone can understand me, it's you."

"At least I've tried," he said tightly. "I suppose if a woman loves a man enough it justifies any deceit or treachery she practices on others."

Belle knew he was referring to the trickery by

which she had saved the Morgans at Galena Crossing and again at Turkey Creek.

She looked away. "I've given you every reason to hate and despise me." It was an effort for her to speak. "I know I must be the greatest fool in the world. But don't scold me, Dick! I—I couldn't stand it! Things happen, and they can't be undone."

Sight of the old home, with Ned standing on the steps to welcome her, was almost too much, and Dick saw her bite back her tears. "You go in," he told her. "I'll sit here on the gallery with Doc."

Wasson spoke to her briefly and led her to the colonel's door. He came back then and sat down beside Marr. His face was long and sober.

"I know better, but seeing her here makes it harder than ever for me to tell myself this isn't some fantastic dream. I asked her to make her peace with her father. But I know it won't amount to anything. You can't expect her to break with Morgan and give herself up."

"Not at once," Dick admitted. "But I believe some good will come of it."

Belle had been with her father more than half an hour when the door opened and she ran out calling for the doctor. After a few minutes Wasson came out of the sickroom alone. "He's gone!" he said soberly. "I guess it's for the best! She wants to be with him for a minute."

"Is she all right?" Dick asked, his gruffness failing to hide his emotion.

Wasson nodded. "Her steel nerves snapped, but she'll be okay. I'll go back and tell old Ned and the rest of them."

Belle's eyes were wet when she stepped out on the gallery. "I guess it's time for me to be going," she said, her voice unsteady.

"You don't have to hurry," Dick urged sympathetically. "You should have some coffee or something before you start back."

She shook her head. "It'll be easier to go now."

They rode down to the river without speaking. Both reined up, knowing this was good-by.

"Why don't you tell me I killed him, Dick?" she demanded self-accusingly. "You know I'm to blame."

"It would be foolish for me to say that, Belle. You hurt him, but his heart has been bad for years. He was an old man."

She shook her head bitterly. "I'll never be able to forgive myself. He asked me to wipe the slate clean and make a fresh start. I promised I would, but I was lying. It would mean giving myself up, going to prison. I'd rather be dead!"

"What else have you got ahead of you if you go on as you are?" he asked. "The law already has one grudge against you. Will a second one, and a third, help you any? You'll be caught eventually— or killed. I have to regard you the same as I do any other bandit. Belle, give yourself up!" he pleaded. "You're a woman. A jury will go easy with you on a first offense. If you get five years, you won't have to serve more than eighteen months. I can arrange to have you sent to a woman's reformatory in Massachusetts. It'll be hard, but it won't be as bad as being committed to a federal penitentiary."

"I couldn't stand it, Dick!" she cried. "You know the kind of women I'd be put with! I made my choice when I ran off with Britt. It's too late to think of turning back. I'll have to face whatever is coming to me. But it won't be prison—I'll never let you take me alive."

"Have you given any thought to what is to become of the ranch? You know Bill will be back to claim his share. If you won't put yourself in a position to protect your interests, how long do you suppose it will be before Bill runs through everything?"

He had played his trump card, but he realized immediately that it wasn't good enough.

"You owe your father something—to keep Woodhall Ranch going!" he drove on, without regard for her feelings.

Belle's chin quivered as she faced him. "So you've turned against me, too! I don't blame you, Dick! But don't crucify me for being a fool." Her eyes were wet. "I'll go! I can't stand any more! I wish you'd bury Father in Guthrie, with Mother."

"I promise you that will be done," he said.

She struck her horse with the quirt and started across the river. She did not glance back, and in a minute or two he lost sight of her in the brakes.

Having lived for days with the knowledge that the colonel was a dying man, Dick found his sense of personal loss blunted, now that the end had come. He was glad he had Doc Wasson to fall back on in this emergency. Doc had found Bill's address.

"He's got to be notified," Doc said. "I'll take care of that and handle the other details here if you will arrange things in Guthrie."

They carried out that arrangement, and Marr took the train down that evening. He was to learn in the next several days that Zach Woodhall in death was a more important figure in the life of Oklahoma than he had ever seemed to be when alive. His passing was front-page news in every paper. To quote the *Oklahoman*, *His passing marks the end of an era that will be long remembered.*

Uncle Ben Small, Gil Skidmore, and their cronies had been able to muzzle the newspapers in regard to Belle and her marriage to Britt Morgan. Now, the floodgates were open, and reporters and feature writers from as far away as St. Louis and Chicago began to arrive in Woodhall and Guthrie. Though Marr and Uncle Ben refused to be interviewed, reams of copy were written about "Belle Woodhall, the Outlaw Queen of the Cimarron." Even before old Zach was in his grave, the headlines were screaming over half the country.

Bill arrived for the funeral. He went almost unnoticed among the great and near-great who came to pay his father homage. He had little to say to anyone, to Dick, in particular. The latter was glad when the ceremonies were over. To him they seemed too elaborate and gaudy for a simple man like Zach Woodhall.

Skidmore, the colonel's lawyer, and Uncle Ben dropped in at Marr's office before taking the train to Oklahoma City. "Maybe the noise and holler will die down, now that Zach is in the ground," the old marshal declared wearily. "It's been a trying time, with all these newspaper people pestering the life out of us. If we just keep our mouths shut, they may head for home without learning that Belle was with her father when he died." It was his only reference to the fact that he knew about it.

"Thank the Lord the colonel was spared all this avalanche of melodramatic trash!" Skidmore exclaimed heatedly. "Dick, when you get back to Woodhall, see Terhune and make him agree to stay with the ranch for the present. I wrote the colonel's will and I'm named executor. Aside from a small bequest to Ned, Bill and Belle share everything. Bill will insist on having the will probated at once. I can't stop that, but I'll do my best for her."

"I'm afraid it won't be enough, Gil!" Uncle Ben pursed his lips pessimistically. "The chief asset of the ranch is the livestock. Somebody's got to be put in charge. Bill will ask the court to appoint him if you raise any objections. He'll most likely have it his way. What sort of shape was Zach in, Gil? Did he owe a lot of money?"

"I suppose he did. He was never a good businessman. He made money with one hand and spent it just as fast with the other. That's one reason why I want Terhune to stick it out for a while."

Dick said, "I'll get Ross to agree to that."

"It's only playing for time," Uncle Ben argued.

"That's right," Skidmore agreed. "Give us a little time and maybe we can do something."

"Do just what?" Uncle Ben demanded gruffly.

"Smash Morgan and take Belle into custody!" Dick interjected, his face suddenly flat and hard.

"That's exactly what I meant!" the lawyer exclaimed.

Chapter Thirteen:
CASING THE LAYOUT

MARR HAD NO DIFFICULTY in getting Terhune's promise to avoid a break with Bill Woodhall and stay on the ranch at least for the rest of the summer.

Contrary to their expectations, days passed without Bill putting in an appearance. Marr learned that he was spending his time in Guthrie and Kingfisher, conferring with lawyers. A day or two later he read that the colonel's will was to be offered for probate. In due course it was accepted by the court and claims against the estate were ordered filed. They were of a size to bring Gil Skidmore to Woodhall at once. He was at the ranch several days going over the colonel's books and papers. He spent an evening with Marr. He took a serious view of the situation.

"It's worse than I had any reason to expect," he said. "There's only one way to satisfy these claims; that's to sell a big slice of the ranch. It's a good range; there won't be any trouble finding buyers. Thad Taylor and Goss will be glad to buy it in. Expenses will have to be trimmed all along the line, too. The colonel's fast horses will have to go for whatever they'll bring."

"What about Bill?" Marr asked. "Has he shown his hand?"

"He can't do anything until the claims are settled, or the creditors agree to let the obligations ride for the present and have him put in charge of the property." Skidmore brushed that possibility aside lightly. "His record is against him; he hasn't a chance of pulling off anything like that. But he's having a try at it, and he has already served a formal request on me to have himself installed as manager of the ranch. He's got a smart young lawyer handling things for him. When the debts have been liquidated, they'll bring me before the court and make me show cause why he shouldn't be put in charge."

"Can you block that move, Gil?" Dick's interest was as frank as it was keen.

Skidmore shrugged dubiously. "I hesitate to commit myself. The situation is without a precedent. He's a principal heir—half owner of whatever estate remains. He'll claim that he can best protect his own interest by being given the authority he seeks. I can prove his unfitness, but what about the other heir—Belle? There's a felony indictment against her; she's living outside the law. I can't offer any evidence that the situation in regard to her will change presently or in the foreseeable future. They'll contend that it won't; that I'm trying to impose a condition that may continue for years, thereby denying Bill Woodhall the right to enjoy and protect his legacy, as his father intended." Gil tossed his cigarette away disgustedly. "They'll be hard to stop!"

"But the liquidation proceedings will take some time."

"Considerable!" Skidmore declared, with a knowing nod. "When I know how much range has to be sold, I'll sell it at public auction. That'll stall things off for thirty days."

Bill arrived on the last day of the lawyer's stay. They had an angry encounter. Skidmore told Marr about it while waiting for his train.

"I've got every dollar tied up, and he's beside himself about it," he said. "I told Terhune he didn't have to take any orders from Bill; that he's my agent and responsible only to me."

"I'm afraid the fur will fly between them," Dick said frankly.

"I don't care if it does," Skidmore chuckled. "I fancy Terhune can take care of himself! Bill can't order him off the place!"

After the train left, Marr walked back to the hotel, the realization strong in him that whatever he was to do had to be accomplished in six to eight weeks, at most.

He saw Terhune in town the following morning. The foreman called him aside.

"I just handed four of the men their time," he began, with a long face. "They were old hands on the ranch. I hated to do it, but Skidmore says we've got to cut down. I suppose you know I'm shipping all the colonel's blooded horses to Oklahoma City in a day or two."

"I understood they were to be sold," said Dick. "I didn't know you were to ship them—"

"Skidmore says they'll bring more down there, and I guess he's right. It's pretty tough to see things going this way. There's three or four darkies on the place that we don't need. I'll have to let them go, but I'll be damned if I'll turn old Ned off. I'm glad the colonel left him a little nest egg."

Marr gave him a tight-lipped nod of approval. "You stick to that, Ross. Old Ned can earn his keep. How are you and Bill making out?"

Terhune gave his Stetson an angry tug. "I don't know how much longer I can hold in! If I have to slap him down, I'll do a good job of it! He's rip-roaring drunk this morning, and when he's liquored he's got a mean tongue!"

"Maybe he won't stay long," Dick suggested. "I imagine he just came up to see what Gil was doing."

Marr ran up to Enid for a day or two to avoid seeing the horses that had carried the Woodhall colors, and that had meant so much to the colonel, shipped away to be sold. When he returned, Huck told him Ri Carver had driven through town, bound home to Bowie.

"Did you speak to him?" Dick inquired.

"Just a word. He said he'd like to see you."

Marr found it important enough to say he'd go to Bowie in the morning. Instead of making the roundabout trip by train, he struck off across country on his big bay and was there by noon.

He had just stabled his horse when he met Carver on the street. "Look me up at the hotel," he said, as they passed.

He had been waiting in his room in the Bowie House only a few minutes when Ri walked in.

"I've been catching up on the news since I got back," the big man said as he sat down. "I got to the Fort too late to keep Belle out of that Wetonka raid. I think I could have done it if I'd been there in time."

Marr regarded him with a puzzled light in his eyes. Ri rewarded him with a dry chuckle. "I figured when I told you I was going back to Rock Creek that you'd surmise I had a reason other than business," he declared. "You knew I'd just covered that territory." He wasn't finished, but he broke off and drummed on the arm of his chair with his fingers absent-mindedly for a moment. "Dick—Belle and Morgan aren't living together as man and wife. She knows she isn't married to him."

Marr straightened up. "How did she find out— through you?" he demanded, not trying to dissemble his surprise.

Ri nodded. "But I was only the mailman. It

came about in a strange way. I'm not in the habit of putting my nose into other people's business. This time, I didn't see how I could otherwise. It's not a long story. I told you Morgan had a Cherokee girl that he claimed was his wife. Her name is Lucy Redbird. She's working in Bartlesville now. Her folks live on the Verdigris, a few miles south of there. She saw something in a Bartlesville paper about Morgan marrying Belle. The first I knew about her getting steamed up over it was when I woke up one morning and found her sitting out on my front porch. She had scraped up money enough to bring her all the way over from Bartlesville. She had her marriage license with her."

"Why did she come to you?" Marr asked, and instantly regretted the question.

"I thought that explained itself," said Ri, a little irked. "She knows my business takes me beyond the Cimarron. She hasn't any feeling against Belle. Morgan kicked her out, and she hasn't forgotten it. She'd cut her heart out to make him some trouble. She'd come to ask me to deliver a letter to Belle."

"Good Lord!" Dick groaned. He got out of his chair and walked to the window and stood staring blindly at the street below.

"I know it was cruel to have Belle hear it that way—but she had to be told," Ri continued. "I felt sure that if she knew, she'd break with Morgan;

178

that wild horses couldn't hold her. At that time, you remember, the Morgans hadn't ridden in to rob that bank at Wetonka. They had just got back from that raid the day before I reached Spanish Fort."

"Just how did you tell her?" Dick questioned, turning away from the window.

"I didn't go right to her. Morgan was in the store with Link and Frank Cherry. I did my talking to him. I told him Lucy had been to see me. He knew what was coming and tried to shut me up. But I told him he was a dirty, low-down rat, and a few other things, I imagine. I wasn't packing a gun; maybe that was just as well. I know Cherry and old Link are bandits, but I've always found a streak of decency in them. I figured if things got too tough, they might take a hand on my side. I can tell you right now that Link Mulvey is the real headman of that bunch today. But I'm getting ahead of myself."

He paused to mop his face. Marr opened a window, saying, "It's close in here."

Carver nodded. "We're in for a hot spell, I reckon. As I was telling you, it slayed Morgan to be told to his face that he was a rat for what he'd done to Belle. He slapped a gun at me, and Link jumped in between us. He told Morgan he better go slow; that I had more friends out there than he did. You know Morgan and how he'd feel about being told where to head in. For a second I thought he was going to blaze away at Link. I don't know whether it was a flash of sense or what it was that stopped him. Anyway, we were snarling at each other, when Belle walks into the store. She'd overheard enough to understand what the argument was about. I figured I might as well let her have the letter."

"Ri, it must have crushed her to get it that way—in front of all of you!"

"Well, it didn't, Dick! It rocked her, but she stood there game as you please and asked Morgan what he had to say about it. He told her he didn't have anything to say—that she could like it or lump it and it would be all the same to him. She asked me what I knew. I said I'd seen the license." Carver shook his head as he relived that moment. "She just exploded then! I've seen Belle when she was mad, but never like that! It wasn't pretty to listen to. If a woman ever gave me the dressing down she gave Morgan, I'd crawl into a hole and rot before I ever showed my face again. I tell you he was scared, Dick! You could see the yellow coming out of him. Arkansaw wasn't there; I don't know how he lines up; but Morgan knew he stood alone as far as Cherry and Link were concerned."

Marr recalled how Link Mulvey had asserted himself that evening in the dugout, when Huck and he were trying to find Ri. Mulvey's voice had been the strong one; not Morgan's. It seemed to confirm Carver's story, coming as it had a few hours after the argument at Spanish Fort.

"What was the upshot of it?" he queried impatiently.

"I begged her to gather up her things and let me take her home. I realized right there that I was licked. Morgan took me up; he told her to clear out; that he was through with her. She said she couldn't go back; that it meant arrest; prison; that she'd sooner be dead. She turned to Link and told him the only place she'd be safe was with him and the rest of the gang. Link hurled his chaw of tobacco to the floor and laid Morgan out worse than she had done. He said Morgan had made her one of them against all the objections Cherry and Younger and he had raised, and she could stick with them as long as she pleased."

Ri slapped his knee with an air of finality and got to his feet. "Dick, you ought to be able to see what the outcome of all this is going to be. You've whittled that gang down to rock bottom. They didn't get much off that Santa Fe train, and little or nothing at Wetonka. They're clawing at one another now, and there's only one thing holding them together. They've got to make a big stake. That's what they're telling themselves. One more big haul before they break up and light out for old Mexico! They'll plan it carefully—Morgan's got the brains for that—and it'll be something out of the ordinary!"

"I can't find any fault with that argument," said Marr. "I believe it hits the nail on the head. When did you leave the Spanish Fort?"

Ri had to think a moment. "A week ago yesterday. I figured that as long as I was out that far and had the wagon full of supplies, I might as well try to find a little business, so I went up as far as the big bend of the Cimarron. I've got to be running along now; the missus will be waiting dinner."

The marshal thanked him for his co-operation. "If you had told me what you were going to do, I undoubtedly would have tried to talk you out of it," he admitted. "That would have been a mistake, seeing how things have turned out."

"I'm glad you feel that way about it," the big man remarked. "I know I'm leaving you with a problem. Trying to put your finger on the spot the Morgans will hit is like trying to find a needle in a haystack. You'll undoubtedly worry your brains out over it, but if you happen to come up with the right answer, luck will have as much to do with it as anything else. You heading back to Woodhall this afternoon?"

"No, I'll go out to the Pot Hook, as long as I'm here, and offer Berthold a settlement on the claim he's made against us for damages to his house. I'll spend the night in Bowie."

"I better not try to see you again," said Ri.

"Don't risk it," Marr agreed.

He sat down by himself after Carver left, his thoughts all of Belle. The future had never seemed so black. Even in his love for her he found it impossible to escape the bitter realization that only arrest could save her now. Knowing the pride that was in her, he pitied her as he never had before. He appreciated the strength of the invisible chains that bound her to the Morgan gang. Despising Britt, she had to cling to him.

The bitter irony of it was like a knife in Marr's flesh. He had a bite to eat before he left for the Pot Hook. His errand there was successful, and by evening he was back in Bowie. He had dinner with Ferd Shapley, the town marshal.

Though Shapley was young, he had made a name for himself. Bowie was large enough to afford an efficient police force, and the marshal had three deputies on full-time duty. Since the Stillings gang had tried to crack the Bowie National, now a matter of six years ago, the town had seen no bandits. The Stillings brothers had been wiped out in that fight, the last gun battle that Uncle Ben Small had to his credit. Shapley had played his part in that fight.

As might have been expected, their conversation largely concerned the Morgan gang. Marr voiced the opinion that they would strike somewhere soon and try to revive their waning fortunes. He said nothing about his talk with Carver.

"If they're out to make a killing, they'll go after a train," Shapley prophesied.

"Or a big-town bank," Marr supplemented, "and I'm not excluding Kingfisher and Enid."

"It might be Blackwell—"

"It could be any one of a dozen places! When a gang gets desperate there's little use in trying to figure what their play is going to be."

He begged off, saying he was tired when Shapley offered to arrange a card game for the evening. He was not too tired, however, to draw a chair up to the window, when he reached his room, and sit there until midnight, making a mental check list of the towns where the Morgans were most likely to appear. Some he could eliminate easily enough, but there were fully a score that held possibilities.

They were all railroad towns with which he was thoroughly familiar. But though he racked his brains, he couldn't single out one place, nor even two or three, with any confidence. Blackwell intrigued his interest. Certain things made it appear to be the most likely spot; and there were other reasons, just as strong, that said exactly the opposite. It was the same with the other towns. Disgusted, he gave up finally and went to bed, telling himself he might better have followed the advice he had given Ferd Shapley.

Sitting here trying to figure out where they'll strike is just as useless as I said it was, he thought. *Guesswork is guesswork no matter what you call it.*

He was awake at an early hour. The sun was streaming in through the front window, and the room was already hot and stuffy. When he lowered the shade he glanced below and saw a man in ministerial garb step out of the hotel and cross the street. In Bowie, as was the case in so many Oklahoma towns, the hotel faced the bank. He noticed the interest with which the bespectacled man in the frock coat and black hat regarded the Bowie National.

It rang a warning bell in Marr's brain. He recalled how Morgan had boasted to Ri Carver that he had dressed himself as a minister at Excelsior Springs and no one had recognized him. With sharpened gaze he stared at the man below. What he saw made him draw in his breath. The man's walk, the cut of his chin, and the aquiline nose left nothing to the imagination. It was Britt Morgan!

Chapter Fourteen:
SQUARING AN OLD GRUDGE

MARR PULLED ON his clothes with feverish haste and ran downstairs and out of the hotel. He knew there was an early morning train to Kingfisher, and he took it for granted that Morgan was on his way to the depot, only a short walk.

Other people were going down to the train. Morgan wasn't in sight when Dick turned the bank corner, but he had hardly expected to see him, being sure he had had time to reach the depot.

The marshal slowed his pace so as not to attract attention. The train wasn't due for a few minutes. If he could catch Morgan buying his ticket, he'd shove a gun into his ribs and Britt would have no choice but to start reaching. Marr half drew his gun to be sure it was free in the holster.

He purposely kept behind a man and his wife on the last few yards to the depot. He let them enter and then stepped in after them. Several people were at the ticket window. Morgan was not one of them, nor was he anywhere in the waiting-room or on the platform.

The train came in. Marr watched the Bowie passengers get on. The conductor called his "All aboard," and the morning local steamed south. Morgan had not taken the train!

He spotted me! thought Dick.

There was another morning train, the north-bound for Manatee, but it was not due for an hour. Morgan would hardly have hurried down to the depot with all that time to wait.

It convinced Marr that the bandit was either in hiding or had left Bowie by team or on horseback. The town had three or four livery barns. The leading one was located on the road that led down to the depot.

Marr hurried back to it. He found two stable-men in the barn. They said they had not seen any minister that morning. Both recognized the marshal and wanted to be helpful.

"You can cross the street and go down that alley to the hotel barn," one told him. "Or you can turn up in back of the bank and git to Krausmeyer's stable."

The hotel barn seemed the more likely place to look, and Marr hastened there. He was equally unsuccessful. There was nothing for him to do but to turn back to the road and go up the alley at the rear of the bank to the other stable. "Yuh," the proprietor told him, "the preacher got his horse half an hour ago."

"Did he say where he was going?" Marr rapped.

"No, he yust rode on up the alley."

With a start such as Morgan had, Dick knew he

was foolish to attempt to overtake him. A little sober reflection made him realize that he had not been left holding the proverbial empty bag. He went back to the Bowie House and had a look at the register. "Rev. Henry Black" had been stopping there for two days. It told Marr in letters that were a foot high that Morgan had been in Bowie sizing up the bank. Nothing else would have held him there that long. He had occupied a front room on the second floor, an ideal point of vantage from which he could acquaint himself with the life of the town and the flow of business in the bank.

Knowing it was still too early to find Shapley at his office, Marr went into breakfast. He felt he had two days, possibly longer, in which to prepare for the raid. Luck, as Ri had said, had proved more important than all the cogitating.

"Just blind luck!" he admitted to himself. "Bowie would have been the last place I'd have looked for the gang to hit. If I had pulled down that window shade last night, I'd never have noticed Morgan."

It lacked a few minutes of eight when he walked into Ferd Shapley's office. The latter looked a little surprised.

"I thought you'd be on your way to Woodhall by now, Dick."

Marr sat down without answering. Something in his gray eyes told Shapley this wasn't any time for levity.

"Ferd, I can tell you where the Morgans are going to show up."

"Yeh?" Shapley queried, not too concerned. "Where?"

"Bowie."

"What!" Ferd Shapley snapped erect in his chair and stared at Marr incredulously. "You don't mean that, Dick!"

"I sure do," was the quiet answer. "Morgan's been in town for two days, sizing up the Bowie National. He passed himself off as a preacher. You may have seen him on the street."

"Good Lord, I did! I saw him in the bank, changing some money. It never crossed my mind that it might be Britt Morgan!"

"Well, you can believe it now," said Marr. "I saw him from my window this morning. I thought he was going down to the train. It took me a few minutes to throw on some clothes and get down to the depot. He wasn't there; he'd left town on horseback. If you've got anything else on your mind, forget it; we've got to get set for this. I'll get word to my men. They'll be drifting in to town sometime this afternoon, with instructions to keep under cover. There doesn't want to be any talk, Ferd. Make your deputies understand that."

The bank corner was the busiest in Bowie. That Morgan would employ his usual tactics of coming in by the side street, posting a couple of men in front of the bank to hold the town at bay while he and one of his gang got busy inside, seemed very unlikely.

"He'll come up with something better than that," Shapley declared. "He must have seen you a dozen times yesterday."

"No question about it. I wouldn't be surprised if he learned what I was doing in Bowie. The only thing that really matters, Ferd, is that he doesn't know I recognized him. I believe he left without even suspecting I'd seen him. Suppose we go up to the bank and look it over."

"Are we going to say anything to Pennyman?" Shapley asked, as they stepped out on the street. Pennyman was the president of the bank. "If we do, he'll tell the cashier, and the tellers will get it next. By noon the story will be all over town."

"We certainly don't have to tell him Morgan is going to attempt to touch up the Bowie National," said Marr. "It'll be enough to say I have reason to believe some bank is going to be stuck up and that I'm looking things over so I can advise you what to do, just in case the Morgans ride into Bowie."

"That's all right as far as it goes," Shapley remarked. "But what's he going to say when he sees you sticking here in town?"

"I don't expect to be showing myself," said Marr. "I'll pretend to leave this noon. I'll lay out for my men to come along. We'll be careful how we ride in. I want you to arrange some place where we can lie low."

After what appeared to be a casual inspection of the bank, the marshal and Shapley walked over to the hotel.

"We'll go upstairs," said Marr. "I want to make a little diagram."

In the room Shapley walked to the front window as Dick looked for pencil and paper. "I can put two or three men up in these rooms and just about make it impossible for anyone to get into the bank," he observed.

"If you do, some innocent people are going to get killed, Ferd. It's all right to put some men up here, but there doesn't want to be any promiscuous shooting. In fact I don't want a shot fired unless it's absolutely necessary, and I don't believe it will be. Let me finish this little drawing and I'll explain what I mean."

There was an open space behind the bank, forming a small back yard. It was closed off from the side street and the alley by an eight-foot-high board fence. On the alley side there was a door. It was always kept locked from the inside. Dick indicated all this in his sketch.

"There!" he said. "I guess that does it. Now I'll tell you how I think Morgan is going to play it. I believe the gang will come up the alley, leave their horses there, with someone to hold them ready, while the rest of them turn up here, on the side street, and walk to the corner. There'll be at least three or four of them. I expect Morgan to walk into the bank with the others at his heels. When they're ready to leave it will be by the back door. It won't matter much whether they've found the key to the door in the fence or not. A shot will blast the lock off. They'll grab their broncs, then race back up the alley."

Shapley nodded soberly. "That could be it," he admitted. "It's simple—and nervy. They would very likely have got away with it if they had caught me by surprise. It was a close call, Dick!"

"We may not be out of the woods yet," Marr reminded him. "You don't have to worry about the alley; my bunch will take care of things there. If I've got Morgan's strategy figured out correctly, we'll grab them as soon as they get out of the saddle. If I'm mistaken, it'll be up to you to stop them."

"What sort of a stand do you want me to make?"

"Cover the side of the bank, Ferd. Do it from the windows of the grocery store opposite. You can put a couple men up here for insurance, but you and your deputies make your fight from the store windows."

Shapley at once signified his readiness to carry out his end of such an arrangement. "Before we go into details," he said, "tell me how much time you think we've got."

"We may have only a few hours," Marr returned, with disconcerting frankness. "It's entirely possible that Morgan may try to pull it off this afternoon. It all depends on where the gang has rendezvoused. They may be within a few miles of Bowie."

Shapley said he doubted it.

"So do I," Marr continued. "But we can't afford to disregard that possibility. It's my guess that the gang has moved up to the Cimarron. If that's the case we won't see them until tomorrow. Friday might suit their purpose better than Thursday; the town will be crowded and the confusion would work in their favor. About the only thing we can be sure of is that when they come it will be between one and three o'clock. I figure they'll make it as late as they can, for they know they'll have a long daylight getaway ahead of them when they finish here. What can you do about keeping us out of sight? There'll be five of us. It may be a wait of two days. We want to be reasonably close to the rear of the bank."

The Bowie town marshal had no immediate proposal, but after making several suggestions that he admitted had no merit, an idea occurred to him that chased the frown from his face. "Why not use the jail?" he asked. "I can put you and your boys in the cells. You'll have beds, and we can sneak in your meals. I've got a puncher locked up. Just drunk and disorderly; no charge against him yet. I can turn him loose and you'll have the place to yourselves."

"That sounds all right to me," Dick told him. "We can turn our horses in with yours."

They soon had the details worked out. Marr went down to the depot and got a wire off to Woodhall. He got his horse then and jogged out of town for several miles. In his wire he had told Lafe and the others to look for him at the Fowler ranch. It was a sizeable outfit, employing a crew of four. When the men came in at noon, Fowler invited him to sit down to dinner.

The features of one of the cowboys had a marked Indian cast. Marr recognized him readily as Jim Blue, a young Osage half blood. He had arrested him once in connection with the plundering of a wrecked freight car but had let him go after holding him a few days. Blue seemed to bear him no malice. After dinner he sat down on an overturned wagon box with the marshal and smoked a cigarette.

"On your way to Woodhall, eh?" he queried aimlessly.

"No, I'm waiting for my men to pick me up," Marr answered. "How long have you been working for Lee Fowler, Jim?"

" 'Bout a year," Blue answered, his eyes as vacant as ever. "It's a good outfit."

Dick nodded. "I'm glad to see you working and keeping out of trouble. You used to be pretty wild as a kid, around Ponca. I don't suppose you've forgotten the time I took you in."

Jim Blue's face thinned tensely. "I haven't forgotten those steel bracelets you put on me, Mr. Marr, and everybody at the railroad depot staring at me!" His tone was suddenly bitter. "You didn't have any reason to handcuff me; I told you I'd go along with you without any trouble."

"Don't feel that way about it, Jim," Dick urged. "I did it more to impress those boys you were running with than anything else. I thought it would be a lesson to them. It worked out that way. I've never had any more trouble with them."

Blue rode off with the rest of the crew. Marr's glance followed him. *That Indian has got a long memory—for some things,* he mused. *He knows he would have gone to the reformatory if I had pressed the charge against him. But he's forgotten that.*

The Fowler house stood within a stone's throw of the Bowie-Woodhall road. It was after one o'clock before Marr saw Huck and the others coming. He rode out to meet them.

"Don't pull up!" he called. "I'll tell you what's up as we ride along. We want to be in Bowie as soon as we can."

What he told them had an electrifying effect on the field marshals.

"By grab, sounds like this is it!" Huck growled. "I hope we're not too late!"

Marr said he'd ride in first; the others were to

come in singly and use the alley in back of the bank to reach Ferd Shapley's barn.

"We can watch the alley from the jail," he added. "If there's nothing doing by the time the bank closes for today, Ferd will show up a few minutes after three and we can get organized for tomorrow."

From the barred windows of the Bowie jail they kept the rear of the bank and the alley under close observation. They had to depend on their ears to tell them what went on at the corner and the main street. A shot would be explanation enough.

The marshal knew his men so well that he sensed the absence of tension in them. It told him they shared his feeling that it was too soon to expect the Morgans.

The clock ticked off the minutes and the town continued its peaceful ways without interruption.

"We can take it easy till tomorrow," Lafe Roberts sang out as the clock struck three.

Shapley came in a few minutes later. "It's working out as we figured," he said. "They'll be here tomorrow—or Friday. Sylvester wanted to know why we were hanging out in his store, Dick. I had to tell him something."

"What did you say?"

"About the same story we gave Pennyman this morning. I told him we'd be back tomorrow and maybe for two or three days. It satisfied him. I brought in a bundle of clean blankets for you

196

boys this noon. Emil and Chuck will be along with some supper later on. We often eat here, so it won't be anything out of the ordinary to see some grub being carried in."

"Don't fuss too much," Dick told him. "We'll make out."

They got through the night and following morning easily enough. By noon they were on edge, confident that they held the winning hand this time and that the next hour or two would spell the end of the Morgan gang. For Dick's sake they did not let Belle's name creep into their conversation, but they were all of the opinion that she would be with the Morgans, though her role might not be any more than to hold the horses. He shared their opinion and tried to keep his lips locked, only to decide that he had to make his position clear.

He said, "I'm certain as you are that we'll be seeing Belle. Morgan has so few men left that he can't hope to pull off this job without her. If I know her at all, she'll be just as dangerous as Link Mulvey or any of the others; she won't ask any quarter for herself, and she won't give any. She's a dead shot. I'd like to take her alive and unharmed, but I don't expect or want you to take any unnecessary chance with her."

Huck and the rest nodded that they understood.

Nerves tightened as they waited. Just before two o'clock two horsemen jogged down the alley.

197

They proved to be just a couple of cowpunchers. In the charged stillness Huck Isbell's breathing was loud and rasping. "What in hell's keepin' 'em?" he growled.

"We've got another hour to go," Marr reminded him. "Don't start busting your britches, Huck. We may not see them until tomorrow."

The hour dragged by with maddening slowness. It failed to bring the Morgans. Marr refused to be discouraged. When Shapley came in he sounded as confident as ever. "They're making it Friday, all right," he said. "They know that most of the farmers and ranchers who'll be in tomorrow will have business at the bank and there'll be a lot of money lying around."

There was more talk in the same vein, but they could not conceal their disappointment. The long wait, with nerves keyed up for a showdown, and the necessity of staying cooped up in the jail, was beginning to tell on them. That night Huck and Lafe got into a wrangle.

"You've got yore opinion and I've got mine!" Isbell growled. "I was as shore as you were that we'd see 'em till that clock in the church struck three! I gave up on 'em right there! We didn't see 'em today and we won't see 'em tomorrow!"

"I'll tell you more about that tomorrow afternoon!" Lafe shot back. "I'm fed up with yore croakin'!"

"Suppose the two of you pipe down and drop

this argument," Marr suggested. "We're sticking this out until something breaks."

The break came early next morning, and it was hardly what Dick expected. Ferd Shapley hurried into the jail a few minutes after seven. The expression on his face was proof enough that his news was bad.

"We've had our trouble for nothing!" he ground out in angry exasperation. "The express office at Magoffin was robbed last night! No one saw the job pulled, but you can be sure it was the Morgans!"

"Why be so sure about it?" Marr demanded, unwilling even now to admit defeat.

"Dick, they were seen within four miles of Bowie yesterday afternoon about one-thirty! They were all set to come in, when they turned back! Somebody tipped them off that we were waiting for them!"

Dick sat down heavily, nonplussed for the moment.

"I knew it!" Huck muttered. "I felt it in my bones!"

Lafe glared him to silence and asked Shapley where he had got his story that the Morgans had been seen close to Bowie the previous afternoon.

"I got it from Jesse Purdy; he just drove into town a few minutes ago," Ferd answered. "He says he saw them below the Bowie-Woodhall road, cutting across Lee Fowler's range. I don't see how the news leaked out; we certainly were careful."

"I think I know how it happened," was Marr's startling admission. "I've got to shoulder the blame for it. I should have had sense enough to realize that when an Indian packs a grudge, he packs it for keeps!" He told them about meeting Jim Blue at the Fowler ranch.

"I reckon that's the answer," said Lafe. "When that Injun saw you meet us and turn back toward Bowie, he was smart enough to put two and two together. It's tough luck. But the Morgans will find we ain't through with them!"

"I guess that's the way to look at it," Dick remarked grimly. "We can't afford to let this get us down. They couldn't have got much at Magoffin, Ferd."

"Just a few hundred dollars. Are you going to slip out of Bowie before the town's stirring?"

Marr smiled mirthlessly. "We better," he said. "It'll help to save your face and mine." He turned to Bryan. "You and Pat go first. Huck and Lafe will follow you in a few minutes. I'll be along then. You wait for me before you reach Fowler's place; we'll turn in there for a minute."

Fowler was about to leave for Bowie when they arrived. "Where is Jim Blue?" Marr asked.

"Why, he ain't here no longer, Marshal! He asked for his time last evenin' and I gave it to him. Somethin' wrong?"

"He'll think so if I ever catch up with him," Dick replied.

They were a silent, sober group as they continued on to Woodhall. Finally little Lafe could hold in no longer.

"I don't know what we got to feel so bad about!" he rapped. "We saved the Bowie National!"

It pulled Marr out of his preoccupation. "Suppose we forget about Bowie," he said. "We're not going back to Woodhall to sit around and wait for the Morgans to have a try at something else. If Uncle Ben will put his okay on it, we're going after them!"

Chapter Fifteen:
WIN OR LOSE ALL

MARR KEPT HIS PLANS to himself as he prepared to go to Oklahoma City. Terhune heard he was back and came over from the ranch to see him. He said Bill Woodhall had gone to Guthrie. "I got by without having to slap him down. But it was just one row after another."

"Have you heard anything further from Skidmore?" Dick asked.

"Yeh, he says we'll have to sell about forty thousand acres of range. That will lop off everything east of the railroad and leave us nothing south and west of Turkey Creek. But I suppose it's got to be done."

He spoke about Belle before he left and said he wished he could feel he was holding the ranch together for her.

"Breaking into the express office in a one-horse town like Magoffin and making off with a couple hundred dollars is pretty small potatoes for a gang of outlaws," he observed. "I suppose Morgan had to show you he could pull another job."

"That's how I see it," said Dick.

He was in Oklahoma City the following afternoon. Uncle Ben sat down with him, and they discussed the Bowie incident at length.

"Don't be discouraged," the old marshal told him. "You can see by what a narrow margin you lost out. You've missed them by inches once or twice before. Just keep it up; you've got the right idea. Sooner or later their luck will run out."

"And so will time," said Marr. "I've always agreed with you that it would be worse than useless to organize an expedition and move out into the Strip and try to round up a bunch of outlaws, but I've come to the conclusion that that's the thing to do with the Morgans."

"No, siree!" Uncle Ben shook his head emphatically. "You could go after them with a hundred men and all you'd accomplish would be to push them back ahead of you! They'll run faster than you can follow, Dick! Ten days after you get back to the Cimarron, they'll be right back where they were when you started out!"

"Not the way I'd play it," Marr insisted. "It will take some careful planning, but it can be done. I know they're located around Spanish Fort. My idea is to block them off in every direction before any attempt is made to close in. I'd need about fifteen men. Fifteen more than I've got, I mean."

"Where you going to get them?" Small demanded irascibly. "I can't spare you another man! You don't mean to swear in a bunch of possemen?"

"I certainly don't. I want real man hunters, men like Eph Logan, Perry, Shapley, and a dozen others who have proved themselves. I know they'll volunteer for the job if their town boards will say the word. And I don't know why they can't be talked into it. If you make the request, what town will say no to you?"

It won a noncommittal grunt from Uncle Ben. He lighted a fresh cigar and leaned back in his chair in thoughtful silence for several minutes.

"I'd throw a circle ten miles wide around the Fort before I began contracting it," Marr argued. "They'd soon know they were hemmed in. When they found they couldn't break through, they'd fall back to the Fort and it would be the Ingalls fight all over again, only this time we'd make a clean sweep!"

"Go on!" Small urged. "I'm listening!"

"I'd have Rufe Perry take a bunch of men around to the north," Marr explained. "The tough job would be to close in from the west. I'd like to have Shapley handle that end. Eph Logan can move in from the east. I'll take my men and head up the North Fork. When the showdown comes, the five of us can handle it."

He talked for half an hour.

"All right!" Uncle Ben snapped. "I'll see what I can do! If the town authorities are willing, I'll let you have your way about it. It doesn't want to be handled with any fanfare. You go back to Woodhall and sit tight for a few days. Time's going to be an important factor. How long do you figure you'll be out?"

"About ten days from the time we cross the river."

Uncle Ben appeared satisfied. "I'll say two weeks. That'll cover it."

Dick's feeling that the various towns would be glad to co-operate was fully justified. Within four days Small was in Woodhall with word that everything was set. "The rest is up to you," he said. "You see Shapley, Rufe, and Logan and make your arrangements."

"I'll wire Rufe and Logan to meet me in Bowie tomorrow morning. I wish you'd come up and sit in with us, Uncle Ben. A word from you may save us from going wrong."

"Well, if you feel that way, I'll be there," Small promised.

The first thing Marr did on reaching Bowie was to get word to Ri Carver to look him up at the hotel. Ri didn't keep him waiting long. "I just saw Eph Logan and Rufe Perry downstairs," the big man remarked.

"Yeh, we're going to have a meeting as soon as Uncle Ben shows up," Dick told him. "There's something I want to ask you, Ri. We're going to need somebody who knows his way around out in the Strip."

"A guide, you mean?"

"Yeh! I can't ask you to go; I know it would be bad for your business. Can you recommend a reliable man? You can surmise what this is all about."

Carver nodded. "What's the matter with Buckskin Charlie Brown? He's old, but he's still as tough as bull-hide. He can find his way around out there with his eyes shut. He must have put in ten years as a government hunter at Fort Supply when it was an army post. He's living in Wahuska with one of his married daughters."

"He'll do fine!" Dick declared. "I never would have thought of old Charlie. I haven't seen him in a couple years. I'll see him tomorrow. And thanks for coming down, Ri."

"That's all right," Carver declared. "I was just going out to my shop to mix up a batch of iron tonic when the boy came with your note." He got up to leave. "I don't want to know your plans, Dick, but be sure you're right before you get in too deep. Things like this have been tried before and never panned out."

"I know it," Marr admitted. "So does Morgan. I'm hoping that will work in my favor."

Uncle Ben arrived within the hour, and the meeting got under way. Marr was pleased with the enthusiasm with which the three men who were to be his lieutenants received his plans.

Shapley was to set out from Kingfisher and continue directly west until he reached the Canadian River and then lead his men to the northwest some 45 miles to the neighborhood of old Fort Supply. It would place him well beyond the outlaw roost. Rufe Perry was to leave Enid, reach the Salt Fork of the Arkansas and follow it out until he was directly north of the Spanish Fort ranch. Eph Logan's contingent would strike west from Wahuska, go through the Galena Hills, cross the Cimarron at Burdette's Ford, and head for the mouth of Rock Creek. Dick and his field marshals would set out from Woodhall, cross the river at once, and proceed up the North Fork.

Dick had brought up a map from the hotel office. He unrolled it on the table and traced the course each party was to follow.

"Ferd will have more riding to do than the rest of us," he said. "I've made a careful estimate of the time it's going to take each one of us to get in position. We'll give Ferd a start of two days before you pull out of Enid, Rufe. Twenty-four hours after you've got started, Eph can leave Wahuska. I'll leave Woodhall as soon as he's well on his way. If we follow that schedule, no one will have to hurry; we can move along slowly and carefully, whip out a lot of country, and be within ten miles of Spanish Fort on the fourth morning after Ferd rides out of Kingfisher."

He turned to Small for his comment. "It sounds all right to me," Uncle Ben declared. "As soon as you start moving you'll lose contact with one another until the fight's on. You better get together on what you're going to do after you start closing in."

"I don't know what you mean by that, Ben,"

Rufe Perry spoke up. "I understand we're to turn 'em back if they try to git through and force them to make their stand at the Fort."

"That's fine if you all understand it that way," the old marshal replied. "I know if one of you happens to find them in front of you and they seem to be on the run, there'll be an awful temptation to force a showdown without regard to what the rest of you are doing."

"That mustn't happen," Marr said flatly. "If we make that mistake, some of them will get away. Each one of us must be able to count on the support of the others. That's the only way we'll have teamwork."

Rufe, Shapley, and Logan agreed that that was true.

Uncle Ben sat back with his cigar, listening carefully and having little to say as they discussed the endless details of the man hunt. He heartily approved Marr's suggestion that Buckskin Charlie Brown be engaged to accompany Shapley. The clock in the Methodist church struck twelve as they sat there.

"Noon!" Uncle Ben announced. "We've talked all morning! There seems to be only one thing left to decide; that's when you aim to start the ball rolling. Let's settle it before we go down to dinner."

"This is Thursday," said Marr. "Two or three days ought to be time enough for any preparations we have to make." He turned to Shapley. "If I have Buckskin Charlie over here by Saturday, can you get your party organized so you can pull out of Kingfisher Monday morning?"

Ferd said yes. Rufe and Logan assured him they could be ready to follow up.

"All right, it's Monday, then!" Dick exclaimed.

"Monday," Small echoed. "See that you stick to it! I don't have to tell you I wish you luck."

Marr saw Buckskin Charlie the next day and found him not only willing but anxious to get out with Shapley.

"Ferd will answer your questions and tell you what he wants after you get started," he informed the old man. "You be in Bowie sometime Saturday."

He borrowed a good pack horse from Terhune and purchased food enough to last ten days. It left nothing to do but wait. On Monday morning he was in Kingfisher and saw Shapley leave. Counting Buckskin Charlie, Ferd had six men in his party.

Two mornings later Marr was in Enid to see that Rufe Perry and his men pulled out on time. He came down to Wahuska then and waited over a day to see Logan's party ride out. That afternoon he led his own men across the Cimarron.

He was no longer interested in trying to pick up information at some dugout. On the contrary, he gave them a wide berth. The weather was fine, for a change. The buffalo grass was already brown. Three months and more had passed since the Morgans had robbed the bank at Manatee.

"How far you plannin' to go today?" Huck inquired.

"Wherever evening overtakes us," Dick answered. "We'll hit the North Fork about five. I just want to be sure we have supper over and our fire out before dark."

He rolled up in his blanket under the stars that night and told himself it was win or lose all for him now. He knew Uncle Ben had gone along with him against his better judgment. If the venture failed, Marr felt he would have to resign his commission. On the other hand, he realized he could capture the Morgan gang and still count it a failure if it put Belle out of his life forever.

They were moving up the North Fork in the morning, when a rider topped a distant rise, took a look at them, and abruptly turned his horse and disappeared at a driving gallop.

"That knocks the secret higher'n a kite!" Lafe burst out. "At the rate that gent's goin' he'll be tellin' his news to Morgan within an hour!"

"I don't think it matters," said Marr. "In fact it may be all to the good."

"How do you figger that?" Huck put in.

"Why, I expect Morgan will gather up his gang and drop back from the Fort when he hears we're coming. If he goes north he'll run into Rufe, and that will jar him, finding he's got trouble moving at him from two directions. If he swings west he'll meet Ferd. About that time he'll begin to realize he's in a fix, and by evening he'll know it for a certainty. We won't get much sleep tonight."

By nightfall they were not more than five miles from the Fort. Marr disposed his men carefully. Sometime after midnight they heard distant shooting, once from the east and the second time from Shapley's direction. Just before dawn Jim Bryan's rifle cracked viciously. He kept on firing until Dick reached him.

"They were sneaking down that little draw in single file!" he asserted. "I could see them above that stand of turkey brush! It's three hundred yards. I don't suppose I mussed them up much."

"That's okay!" Marr exclaimed approvingly. "You turned them back! That's all we want to do for the present. I'll move over east of you a bit. It'll be light in a few minutes."

Dawn came on, and they saw nothing more of the bandits. Huck was openly optimistic at breakfast.

"By grab, I actually believe we got 'em cornered!" he declared. "I don't know what this day is goin' to bring, but I got a feelin' it's goin' to be remembered!"

They knew that every clump of brush held a possible ambush now, and they moved up cautiously. Pat Curry was first to catch sight of riders moving up, off to the west. "It's Shapley's bunch!"

Marr studied the distant horsemen for several minutes. They were too far away to be recognized, but their methodical advance left no doubt as to who they were. "It's Ferd all right!" he said, a blessed feeling of relief whipping through him. He had never doubted that Rufe would be able to close in from the north and Logan from the east; he had been less confident about the western sector of the circle. He felt trouble was most likely to be encountered there, and it was for that reason he had assigned Ferd, young and vigorous, to it. If he had come through, there was no reason to worry about the others, he told himself. Fortified and confident, he led his men forward.

Chapter Sixteen:
A FIGHT TO THE FINISH

ANOTHER FORTY MINUTES brought them close to the Rock Creek bottoms. A horseman rode out of the brush and hailed them. It was Eph Logan. "We've been standing on the creek for some time," he announced, as Marr rode up. "We heard some gunfire at dawn. We figured you were having a brush with them."

"Bryan spotted them," Dick told him. "You must have run into them last night."

"We did," was Logan's laconic answer. "They saw us coming, dark as it was, for they'd hauled off into a patch of brush. One of their broncs nickered and gave them away. When we opened up on them, they turned tail and ran after exchanging half a dozen shots with us."

The marshal told him they had seen Shapley. "It leaves only Rufe to be accounted for. You haven't seen anything of him?"

"No, but I imagine he ain't far from the Spanish Ranch. There's something stirring up there. We saw a couple riders racing into the Fort."

It was the first positive indication that the gang had been caught in the net.

"We'll keep on moving and draw the string tighter," Marr said. "We're not more than three miles from the Fort right now. Our plan was to pull up as soon as we got in sight of the buildings and wait until we had made contact with one another. We'll stick to that."

"Morgan may decide to make his stand at the ranch," Logan observed as they were parting.

"We can depend on Rufe to find out about that, Eph. He won't put the house behind him till he's given it a good going over. It's my guess that the Mehaffeys will sidestep this showdown; they've got their own game to play."

The course Rock Creek took made it necessary for them to keep it in between them, and after Logan turned back into the bottoms, Marr and his men saw no more of the sheriff's party until they were within 400 yards of the two buildings at Spanish Fort, always referred to as the grocery and the hotel. The two sunbaked, weary-looking structures stood naked and alone on the prairie, with only a few feet separating them. The marshals studied them carefully and failed to find any sign of life. They were not deceived by this counterfeit tranquillity.

"Reckon you'd git yore hair curled if you tried to ride in!" Huck observed, with a grim chuckle. He glanced at Marr. "How do you figger we're goin' to do it?"

"By keeping them so busy in four directions at once that they won't know from which side the real fight is coming."

Isbell shook his head dubiously. "It's goin' to be tough! The last seventy-five yards is goin' to be awful tough! If they fort up on the top floor of the hotel they can run from window to window and jest about call their shots!"

Lafe got Dick's attention. "Looks like this is Ferd Shapley comin' down the crick."

It proved to be the Bowie marshal. "Well, we made it!" Ferd exclaimed triumphantly as he rode up. "How did the rest make out?"

Marr told him he had seen Logan and that they were waiting for Perry. "How close up are you, Ferd?"

"About the same as you are. We've got them covered. They're in the grocery. Must be about ten people in there, counting a kid. Old Charlie scouted in pretty close just about daylight. He says the kid belongs to the Frenchman who owns the place."

"Arquette?"

"Yeh, Pete Arquette! Charlie claims there's a couple women with them—Arquette's wife and Belle Woodhall."

"And who else?" Dick asked, his mouth hard.

"Charlie doesn't know. I suppose they're just a couple of punks of the sort you'd expect to find hanging out here."

At Marr's suggestion, Shapley and he rode around to have a word with Logan. The sheriff was talking to a heavy-set man on a white horse. It proved to be Rufe Perry.

"I was just goin' to look you up," Rufe told Marr. "I lost some time with the Mehaffey brothers. I made sure there wasn't no one concealed there. That house was an arsenal, Dick! I gathered up every gun I could find and dumped 'em in the well. I don't suppose I had the authority to do it, but I was damned if I was going to take a chance on leavin' that artillery layin' around!"

"Right!" Marr declared, with hearty approval. "Let the Mehaffeys squawk to me if they don't like it. I'll jug them for harboring outlaws. We better get our heads together now and make sure we know what we're going to do."

He recounted what Ferd had told him.

"Where have they got their hosses?" Rufe asked.

"Old Charlie says they're under the hotel," Shapley replied. "He claims they rode them in at the rear. There must be a cellar."

"I never heard there was," said Marr. "But it's entirely possible. I'm positive it'll be just a question of time before they make a break for their horses. When we drive them out of the grocery they'll run to the hotel. You'll be in the best position to stop them, Rufe. Drop them if you can!"

It lacked a few minutes of eight. At eight-thirty they were to launch what was to appear to be a concerted attack, sweeping to within several hundred yards of the grocery, their gunfire directed at doors, windows, and whoever happened to show his face. They were to swing back, then, re-form their line and repeat the performance, and keep on repeating it until the cornered gang was bewildered. In the meantime Dick and his field marshals were to seize the most favorable opportunity that offered and fight their way into the store.

Soon after the first attack began someone waved a white flag from a front window. A few minutes later Pete Arquette, the squat owner of the hotel and grocery, stepped out of the front door of the store, holding the flag above his head. He was accompanied by his wife and son and two men.

Marr waited until they had reached the creek before he confronted them. The Frenchman protested excitedly that he was a noncombatant. "I don' wan' ma family to git keel in dis fight! She's none of ma beezness!"

"Who are these two gents you've got with you?" Marr demanded suspiciously.

"Dey're just a couple boy what git into some leetle troub', in Texas. Dey don' mak' no troub' here."

"A little rustling trouble, I guess," Dick muttered. He looked the two men over carefully. "All right!" he decided. "Give me your guns and get across the creek and stay there till this thing's over!"

"Dose buildin', Marshal—don' smash dem up too much!" Arquette whined.

"I'll burn them down if that becomes necessary," Dick snapped. "They haven't served any honest purpose in years! If you want to save them, go back and get Morgan to give up."

"Bagosh, *non!*" the Frenchman burst out emphatically. "Morgan don' lissen to dat gal a second tam!"

Belle! Dick thought. He had wondered why Morgan had let Arquette and the two rustlers go, for, at worst, they might have been some little help to him. He understood now.

The Frenchman gathered up his son and carried him across the creek. His wife raised her skirts and waded over after him.

A signal from Marr set a second attack in motion. Knowing the Morgans had to make their stand alone, and that they numbered only five, made it doubtful that they could hold out for long, expert shots though they were. But when Marr and his field marshals raced in, ready to leap from their saddles and dash into the grocery if they got near enough, they ran into a murderous hail of slugs. They were forced to turn back, Pat Curry with the top of his ear shot off, and congratulating himself that he was still alive, and Marr with his sleeve soaked with blood from a bad flesh wound high on his left arm.

The wind was booming down from the

northwest and kicking up clouds of dust around the two buildings, where no grass had grown for years.

"They smelled the rat!" Lafe got out savagely, as he tied up Dick's arm. "We got all of it that time!"

"We'll try another way, this trip!" Marr gritted his teeth as Lafe tightened the bandage. "We'll quarter up on the hotel and be close to the grocery steps before they can open up on us."

They got in close enough, but in the face of the blazing guns that met them it would have been suicide to do anything but flash past the store. The gang had barricaded the windows and door. It ended any chance of rushing them.

Jim Bryan's horse was so badly wounded it had to be destroyed. He put his saddle on the pack horse.

"We could try the back door," Pat Curry suggested.

"If we do we might as well tell them they don't have to bother about Rufe's bunch; that we're the ones to watch," Marr objected.

"They know it already!" Lafe insisted. "Logan and Rufe and Ferd slapped a hundred slugs into the buildin' that time without drawin' an answer. The only way to finish this off is to tell 'em to stop feintin' and really git in there!"

"I can't do it, Lafe," Dick said, as he watched a big tumbleweed bound across the prairie and fetch up alongside the store, where three or four others had lodged. "That wasn't Uncle Ben's proposition to the various towns. Rufe and the rest of them were to help us round up the Morgans; we were to do the fighting. But we aren't stopped. I think I see how we can run them out. We'll do what we should have done at Ingalls; burn the buildings!"

"Will you tell me how yo're goin' to set 'em afire?" Huck put in.

"Yeh! Just watch those tumbleweeds and sage-brush piling up alongside the grocery. There'll be enough of them there in an hour to make quite a blaze. I'll have Ferd pull up some and help things along. The wind's carrying them across in the same general direction every time. We may have to light a few before we get one to pile up against the others and get them burning, but we can do it with a little patience."

He rode around to Shapley and explained his plan. They pulled up some dry tumbleweeds and saw them go bounding away. Fully half came to rest at the side of the store.

"Watch the course they take," Marr advised. "It'll help you when you start some burning ones on their way. Keep sending them across until ten o'clock. That'll be definite and give the rest of us a chance to be ready for whatever happens."

Marr found Rufe anything but impressed by this bit of strategy.

"Sounds foolish to me!" he grumbled. "We've

got men enough to swarm over that bunch! We can do it if you'll just say the word!"

Dick shook his head. "I won't consider it until everything else has failed. You know why I'm saying it. This trick will work. It won't be long after the grocery starts blazing before the hotel will catch. It'll be up to you and your men to stop them when they come tearing out of the cellar. No telling which way they'll try to go, but you'll see them first."

Eph Logan was not given to mirth, but he chuckled when he heard Marr's scheme. "Don't know why it won't work," he said. "The wind's strong enough to set things going in a hurry, once they catch."

The marshal rejoined his men with time to spare. Shapley's group had been busy. Little Lafe voiced a grunt of satisfaction every time a tumbleweed joined the growing pile. Several searching shots, fired at random, came from the grocery.

"Gittin' nervous!" Huck commented. "They're wonderin' what's up!"

Promptly at ten o'clock they saw a blazing bundle of fire come bouncing across the wind-swept prairie. To their dismay it burned itself out before it reached the building. The same thing happened a second and a third time. The next thing they saw was Ferd Shapley, dashing out of some low brush, a flaming tumbleweed in his hand. He raced toward the grocery and cut the distance down to 100 yards before he tossed the blazing torch into the air. Someone fired at him from a window, but he got back safely.

"That did it!" Lafe yelled, as the flames leaped up the warped siding of the building. "She'll be a roarin' furnace in a couple minutes!"

The flames spread rapidly. Marr and his men were gazing at them with fascinated attention when a series of shots rang out. They realized instantly that the gang was dashing to the hotel; that Perry's bunch had not been caught napping.

"Eight shots I counted!" Lafe exclaimed. "All of 'em couldn't have missed!"

"No," Marr muttered, breathing a silent prayer that Belle had not been shot down. "Even if they made it, they must know they won't be safe in there but a few minutes."

The words were barely off his tongue when Rufe's rifles cracked again. Around the corner of the hotel, streaking for the creek bottom, came three of the gang. At first glance Marr was only sure that Belle was one of them. He could see her red hair streaming. For once she was riding astride. And then he saw it was Morgan and Link Mulvey who were with her.

The move caught Marr's contingent by surprise, for they had agreed among themselves that when the gang made a break it would be an attempt to get through to the north or east.

It took the marshals only a few seconds to run to their horses and swing into the saddle. In that brief time one of Logan's men (they learned later that it was Clem Rossiter, the Wahuska town marshal) charged toward the fleeing bandits. His first shot killed Morgan's horse. Britt leaped clear and got to his feet, running. Mulvey and Belle waited for him at the creek, their rifles spitting fire. As Morgan reached Belle, she kicked her feet out of the stirrups and moved back so he could swing up in front of her. It took but a second.

Old Link sat there, with the slugs whining about his ears, and let them get started before he raced after them. He was fearless, without nerves, but his luck had run out. A slug from Huck Isbell's rifle slapped into him and knocked him out of the saddle. It put Link's lawlessness behind him forever.

Morgan and Belle faded into the willows and got across the creek, hotly pursued. Britt was quick to realize that the horse, carrying a double burden, was being outdistanced. He didn't hesitate about what to do. It was a simple matter to break Belle's hold and pitch her to the ground. Marr, 300 yards away, groaned as he saw her plunge out of sight into the brush.

Morgan's horse, its burden lightened, gathered speed. Then, in a surprise move, he turned into the brakes and recrossed the creek.

"He's making for the Spanish Ranch!" Huck shouted.

"You and the boys stay with him!" Dick ordered. "Lafe and I'll take care of things here!"

When he and Lafe got down they could find no trace of Belle.

"Are you hurt, Belle?" Marr called. "Where are you?"

Getting no answer, Lafe and he plunged into the brush. Dick found her. She was sitting up, half dazed, her rifle in her hands. She started to raise it, only to let it drop back.

"I can't do it!" she gasped. "I can't kill you, Dick!"

He knelt down at her side. "Are you hurt, Belle?"

She shook her head. "Just stunned a little." She searched his eyes. "What are you going to do with me?"

"I'm going to have Lafe take you in—get you away from here as quickly as he can. I give you my word there won't be any handcuffs or crowds to gawk at you if you'll just promise to go along quietly."

"No!" she cried hysterically. "You can't send me in! I won't go! I'd rather a hundred times you killed me!"

"Belle, you've had things your way for a long time; it's my turn now," Marr said firmly. "There's only one way you can square yourself, and you're going to do it. All you've got to decide is how you want it done. I'm prepared to put the irons on you and drag you in as I would any outlaw."

"You wouldn't dare!" Her green eyes flashed with their old fire.

"There's nothing I wouldn't dare for your sake, Belle."

Disheveled though she was, her face scratched and her dress torn, he thought only how lovely she was. She sat up, gazing at him for a long moment.

"You can say that—knowing what you do about me, Dick?" she murmured incredulously.

"Yes, Belle," he said simply.

Strangely her eyes began to mist. "All right, Dick; I'll go with Lafe." She buried her face on his knee, crying softly. "Did Morgan get away?"

"Not if that shooting means what I think it does," Marr answered.

When he rode into the yard at the Spanish Ranch he found a dozen men there, including Logan and Rufe Perry. They had their attention fixed on the second floor of the house.

"Where are Bryan and Curry?" he asked Huck.

"Inside! We got Morgan treed this time! Rufe says Cherry and Arkansaw was barely able to crawl out of the hotel, they was so shot up! We'll git Morgan, and that'll be all of 'em!" He was excited, even jubilant. "You want to watch them upstairs windows! He'll jump, when Jim and Pat git close to him!"

They were to be his last words, for as he hurried toward the front of the house, Morgan fired at him from a corner window.

Rufe and several others ran to pick up Huck. Dick kept his attention fixed on the window. He knew Huck was dead. With iron will he closed his mind to it and waited. When Morgan jumped, he put three bullets into him, any one of which would have been fatal.

The fight was over. Marr knelt down and closed Huck's eyes, emotion choking him.

"We didn't miss any of 'em," he heard Rufe say. "Morgan and Mulvey killed; Arkansaw, Cherry, and Belle captured. I reckon this is the end of organized outlawry in Oklahoma!"

"Yes," Marr muttered in bitter anguish as he gazed at Huck's homely, familiar face, "and we paid a high price for it!"

Chapter Seventeen:
IN LIFETIME LEGAL CUSTODY

BUCK YOUNGER, his leg still in a cast, found the monotony of life in the federal jail in Guthrie agreeably relieved with the arrival of the other living members of the Morgan gang, though for several days it was debatable whether Cherry and Arkansaw were to be counted among the living.

The jail had no special quarters for women. Marr did what he could to make Belle comfortable. She was dull and dispirited, and it was only at Dick's insistence that she agreed to ask Skidmore to defend her. Gil came up at once and spent several days conferring with her.

Guthrie was overflowing with newspapermen again. They had little interest in old Buck, or Arkansaw and Cherry, but they tried every stratagem that occurred to them to get an interview with Belle. One of them learned of Marr's romantic interest in his "fair prisoner" (to quote an often-used phrase), and he immediately found them dogging his steps. His patience wore out after two days of badgering, and though his wounded arm was still bothering him, he retaliated by dousing one tormentor in the horse trough in front of the hotel. And no one got to see Belle.

Bryan and Curry had returned to Oklahoma City and been assigned to other work by Uncle Ben. Huck's passing had left such a void in Marr's life, and Lafe's, that he preferred not to have the vacant post filled for the present.

"There'll never be no one like him," Lafe said more than once. "He could be cussed, and stubborn as a mule, but he was always there when you needed him most."

Bill Woodhall seemed to be dividing his time between Guthrie and Oklahoma City. He also seemed to be well supplied with money. It was Gil Skidmore's opinion that he had talked someone into making him a loan against his inheritance.

"Lord knows he must have run through what his father gave him some time ago," Skidmore asserted. "Has he made any effort to see Belle?"

"No, he hasn't been near her," Dick replied. "It's just as well; she doesn't want to have anything to do with him. I heard today that notice of the auction had been posted at the Kingfisher County courthouse."

"It's been up a couple days. The range will be sold at ten o'clock in the morning of July 28 on the courthouse steps. I hope I can be there."

They were seated in the dining-room at the hotel, having supper.

"That's barely two weeks away," Dick remarked. "I don't know why you shouldn't be in

Kingfisher; Belle won't be going to trial before the middle of September."

Skidmore started to answer and then checked himself as Bill Woodhall and some acquaintance of his from Oklahoma City entered the dining-room. He was well jingled, as usual. He had a contemptuous glance for Marr and the lawyer as he passed their table.

"I wonder if you realize what a pleasure it would be for me to wring that pup's neck?" Gil muttered fiercely. "You were speaking about the trial, Dick. I don't want Belle to stand trial with Younger and the rest of them. And for a couple reasons. It will not only drag along for weeks, but it will hurt her chances. Hardesty's got a flock of indictments against Younger, Cherry, and Arkansaw. There's only the one charge against Belle that will stick; the Government hasn't any real evidence so far that she took part in the robbery of the express office at Magoffin."

Marr was well acquainted with Tom Hardesty, the U. S. district attorney. "How does he feel about it?" he asked.

"Oh, Tom is inclined to be reasonable. In fact, he's as good as told me he'd accept a plea of guilty on the Wetonka robbery and drop the other charge. He knows popular feeling is almost unanimously for Belle. I don't mean to say he'd let that sway him; but he's in politics and he's got his eyes open. I spent an hour with Belle this afternoon, trying to persuade her to plead guilty. I told her frankly that she's got nothing to lose. She can't beat the case; Hardesty can put a couple dozen witnesses on the stand who saw her taking part in that robbery. The best I could get her to do was to promise to think it over." Gil shook his head in a baffled way. "I can't understand her!"

"I think I can," said Dick. "It's her pride—and the hope that a miracle will happen."

"There won't be any miracle if a jury has to decide her fate! The best we can hope for is a verdict of guilty with a request for leniency. If it's put up to the judge that way, he'll just about have to give her five years. What I'm trying to do is to take her before Judge Crockett, enter a plea of guilty, and avoid a trial. I know he can be stern; but there's a lot of human kindness in George Crockett. And he understands Oklahomans. He knows damned well there's mighty few of us who haven't made a misstep sometime in our lives. I believe she'd get off with a year or eighteen months."

"It wouldn't help any if I tried to sway her." Marr spoke with a deep understanding of Belle. "Lord knows I would do anything to help her; but this is something she must decide for herself."

"I agree with you," Gil admitted. "I'm going to see her again in the morning."

Dick was at his desk just after breakfast, when Lafe Roberts hurried into the office. "Did you hear about Bill Woodhall?" he asked, obviously hoping the answer would be no.

"What's he done?" Dick inquired obligingly.

"He and some friend of his drove out on the road to Oklahoma City about five this mornin'. They'd been drinkin' all night. You know that stretch where the road runs alongside the Sante Fe tracks?"

"Yeh."

"Wal, when the Chicago Express came through, Bill tries to race the train. The team ran away and pitched both of 'em out. Bill's neck was broken."

"He's badly hurt, eh?" Dick questioned, his interest sharp enough now.

"Hurt?" Lafe echoed dispassionately. "They got him over in Perrine's undertaking parlor! He's dead! And it's one of the best things ever happened around here, if you ask me!"

"And yet they say a drunken man never gets hurt," Marr remarked, getting to his feet and walking to the open door. "There'll be few to regret his going. I'll have to tell Belle."

"It won't mean anythin' to her, Dick. If he'd been halfway right, things might have been different at Woodhall Ranch."

Marr nodded; he felt it was true.

He went back to Belle's cell. She had had some clothes sent down from the ranch and kept herself well groomed. Save for a slight tightening of her mouth she betrayed no emotion on hearing what he had to say.

"If you want to see him, I can arrange it," he offered. She said no.

"I don't have to pretend I'm sorry to you, Dick. You know what Bill was. I can forgive him for the way he treated me, but he hurt Pa—not the way I did—but he shamed him with his drinking and worthlessness. I suppose he'll be buried in the family plot. That's all right; he can't hurt anyone now."

Gil Skidmore made no bones about what he thought of Bill Woodhall's unexpected demise. "Getting killed is the biggest favor he ever did anyone!" he insisted. "With that pup out of the way I can settle the colonel's estate without any trouble—and it'll all belong to Belle someday."

He had a long talk with her. His face was radiant when he came back to the office. He said, "She's agreed to it, Dick! I'll see Hardesty this morning. Judge Crockett will be back from the city by Friday. If everything goes all right we'll take Belle before him Friday afternoon."

Guthrie did its duty by Bill Woodhall and saw him buried quickly and quietly, and with the expressed hope that he would be promptly forgotten.

Uncle Ben had been in town four or five times recently. He never failed to spend a few minutes with old Buck and Cherry and rawboned Arkansaw Bob. Though they had been thorns in his flesh for years, and they, for their part, knew the law he represented was about to send them away for twenty years or more, these meetings were not only free of any trace of enmity but provided an opportunity for reminiscence that both sides found enjoyable.

The old marshal appeared in Guthrie a few hours after Bill had been laid away. He had made up his mind, he told Dick, that the time had come for him to retire. "You know I want you to take my place," he said. "I believe in striking while the iron's hot. You've made a big reputation for yourself, and there's no reason why we shouldn't take advantage of it. But politics are politics! I don't want to depend just on my recommendation to the President. When you can, come down to the city, and we'll get some influential men to back us up."

Marr expressed his gratitude, but somehow it didn't mean as much to him as it once would have done. More and more he had come to feel that his life was empty and meaningless. Even though Belle was a prisoner, confined in a steel cell, he was near to her and able to make her confinement bearable. He knew she would be going away soon. He wondered how he was to go on. Fantastic plans for saving her flashed through his mind and were dismissed as quickly as they were born. One thing occurred to him, however, that wouldn't be brushed aside, and when it became definite that Belle was to appear before

Judge Crockett on Friday afternoon, he acted on it without con-sulting her.

Only Hardesty, the U. S. district attorney, Skidmore, a clerk, and the bailiff were in the courtroom when he walked in with Belle.

"This won't take long," he told her. "I'll have something to say, Belle. Don't be too surprised by it. I'll mean every word of it from the bottom of my heart."

Hardesty read the charge against her, when the judge had taken the bench. Crockett turned to Gil and asked him how his client desired to plead. Gil said, "Guilty, your honor."

The judge glanced at Belle. In a hushed whisper she repeated the one word, "Guilty."

Skidmore made no impassioned plea for mercy. Instead, he confined his remarks to pointing out that Belle was a first offender and had otherwise led an exemplary life. He said she was aware of the serious nature of her transgression, and that she was contrite and wanted to regain the esteem and respect in which she had once been held.

"The prosecution accepts the plea of guilty and joins in asking the court for clemency," Hardesty stated. "The prisoner has not only relieved the Government of the expense of prosecuting her, but I feel there is every reason to believe she desires to lead a useful and law-abiding life."

Crockett removed his spectacles and glanced down at Belle. His demeanor was stern. Marr had seen hardened criminals cower when they faced him.

"Young woman, you bear a respected name," he said, and his tone was not unkind. "I knew your father. He made a great contribution to the settling and building up of Oklahoma. I wish I could be guided solely by that. Unfortunately, robbery with a deadly weapon is a crime, and there is no excuse for it, whatever the circumstances. In your case, however, I don't think the ends of justice demand that you be sentenced to a long term of years. I want to see you take your place again as an honored, respected citizen."

He went on in that vein for some minutes, condemning outlawry and paying tribute to Marr for breaking up the Morgan gang. "We are indebted to you, Marshal. Due to your intrepid courage those bandits have been brought to the end of their bloodstained trail."

Dick saw a dry sob shake Belle. He reached out and pressed her hand encouragingly as the judge called Gil and Hardesty to the bench for a whispered conversation. Whatever it was that Crockett said to the two lawyers, they nodded affirmatively and stepped down. After another of his searching glances at the prisoner, the judge said, "Belle Woodhall, in view of the plea of the Government attorney and defense counsel and the public feeling in your behalf, I sentence you to be confined in a federal institution for a period of eighteen months, subject to time off for good conduct. I shall be glad to accept the advice of the U. S. Marshal's office on where you are to serve your sentence."

Belle winced, but she did not break down. In the charged stillness of the empty courtroom Marr raised his voice. "Judge Crockett, I would like to address the court. I've always regarded whatever I did to put down lawlessness as my duty and not deserving of special thanks. But if I have any consideration due me, I want to ask for it now. If Miss Woodhall did me the honor of becoming my wife, would you suspend sentence and parole her in my custody, Judge? Not for eighteen months, but for life!"

Belle stared at him amazed, speechless. Crockett was so startled his spectacles dropped unnoticed. Hardesty tried to look undisturbed, but his eyes were round with surprise. Skidmore was the only one who took it in stride.

Dick pulled out a paper. "I have a license here," he said, "and a ring. You could marry us now, Judge."

Crockett finally found his tongue. "Well, I can't promise to put her in your custody for life," he declared, his judicial tone forgotten. "That part of it will be up to you, Marshal Dick." He leaned down toward Belle. "I'd like to hear what you have to say about it?"

"I'll marry him—if he'll have me—no matter

what you decide!" she cried, emotion choking her. She turned to Marr and buried her face on his shoulder.

Crockett shook his head indulgently, as though he were some father confessor, and began to smile. He pulled himself up abruptly, however. "Good Lord, I haven't performed a marriage ceremony in so long I've forgotten how it goes!" He flashed a testy glance at Hardesty. "Tom," he snapped, "find me something, so I can brush up; Marshal, you take Miss Woodhall into my chambers. We'll be in in a few minutes."

Belle raised her eyes, shy and embarrassed, when the door closed and she found herself alone with Marr. Suddenly, then, she was in his arms, her eyes wet, but happy and excited.

"Dick! Dick!" she cried. "You've never failed me! Why did it take all this madness and misery to make me realize the truth? It was always there—so plain for me to see!"

She pulled his head down and her lips found his.

"Never let me go!" she pleaded. "I'm going to need you so!"

"We can go away—if that will make things easier for you," he said tenderly. "I won't mind going back to ranching. We can find a place somewhere."

"No, Dick! Uncle Ben told me why he came to see you the other day! Your place is here, and so is mine. I don't want to go away—just home! I want to fight my way back among people who know me. I can do it—with you to help me!"

"I know you can!" he murmured fondly. "We'll go home to Woodhall Ranch this evening. I'll wire Ross we're coming. Old Ned will be there to welcome us, and somehow, I feel the colonel will be waiting for us, too."

Center Point Large Print
600 Brooks Road / PO Box 1
Thorndike, ME 04986-0001 USA

(207) 568-3717

US & Canada:
1 800 929-9108
www.centerpointlargeprint.com